Not Always
Happenstance

Not Always Happenstance

Rachael Anderson

USA TODAY BESTSELLING AUTHOR

HEA Publishing LLC

ISBN: 978-1-941363-15-7

Published by HEA Publishing

for Jeff,
my perfect match

Other Books by Rachael Anderson

Novels

Working it Out
The Reluctant Bachelorette

Meet Your Match Series
Prejudice Meets Pride
Rough Around the Edges Meets Refined
Stick in the Mud Meets Spontaneity

Novellas

Righting a Wrong
Twist of Fate
The Meltdown Match

chapter 1

Time to go.

Easton shoved the last of his toiletries in his travel bag and walked through the small, one-bedroom apartment to make sure he hadn't forgotten anything. Laptop, check. Phone in his pocket. Drawers empty, nothing under the bed, bathroom cabinet clear.

He glanced around the room one last time before he slung his laptop bag over his shoulder, picked up his large duffle, dug the keys to his rental car from his pocket, and opened the door to pouring rain. It came down in sheets, blurring the normally lush, tropical gardens that surrounded the tiny cottage he'd called home for the past three months.

Apparently Sao Miguel wasn't happy to see him go.

Squinting through the murk, he took a deep breath and bolted in the direction he'd parked the car. A push of the remote button caused his headlights to blink, and the trunk popped open. He tossed everything in the back, slammed it closed, then ducked inside, pulling the driver's door behind him. His shorts and hoodie were soaked and would probably remain that way for a while.

Only then did he see a little blue Peugeot parked directly in front of him, blocking the only way out.

"Going somewhere, *meu xodó?*"

Easton jumped and swung his gaze to the side. Samah sat in the passenger seat, arms folded, back straight, jaw taut. Her dark brown eyes fumed at him through the gloomy, early-morning light. She looked as put-together as she always did: long, wavy black hair, pullover top, skinny jeans, and heeled sandals. But instead of the easy smile she usually wore, her plush, kissable lips had tightened into a straight, angry line.

Easton looked away and ran his hand across the back of his neck, giving it a quick massage. He'd begun traveling at the age of twenty, and after eight years of experience, he'd learned that goodbyes should be treated like an expired passport—avoided at all costs. They were awkward, uncomfortable, and when a woman was involved, typically tearful and dramatic, though he didn't understand why. Each and every woman he'd dated had known from the beginning that he didn't plan to put down roots—at least not deep ones. That was one of the reasons he never let relationships move beyond a certain point. When it was time for him to leave, he needed to be able to uproot himself easily and move on. Staying was never an option.

Unfortunately, no matter how clear he tried to make that, the few goodbyes he'd attempted earlier in his travels had ended in disaster. When Mali from Thailand had served him a sharp slap to the cheek and threatened to send her father after him, Easton had decided that goodbyes weren't for him. It was so much easier and less painful to leave the way he'd come—quietly, without fanfare, incident, or emotions.

How had Samah known he was leaving this morning? How long had she been sitting in his car? He probably should have locked the doors, but the near-zero crime rate in the Azores had gotten him out of the habit, not that it would have mattered if he had. Her car now blocked the only exit, so a confrontation would have happened regardless.

"Well?" the shrill voice came again, her Portuguese accent stronger than before. Samah was beautiful, passionate, and adventurous. It's what had attracted him to her in the first place. Her small and lithe body could scurry up and down mountains, leap from the tops of waterfalls, and dive deep below the surface of the ocean. Those petite arms could wind around him in a way that made kissing her its own adventure. His time with her had been the equivalent of a thrill ride. Exciting and exhilarating but now . . . over.

"Samah, you knew my visit here was only temporary," Easton tried, hoping her hands would stay where they were—tucked under her arms.

They didn't. They flew into the air in a dramatic gesture. "You like to see the world for . . . *pesquisa*. *Si*, I know." Although Samah had a strong grasp of the English language, many words still eluded her, like "research." Easton had filled in the blanks and translated for her more than a few times over the past few months. It was one of the things that had attracted Samah to him. Win-win, right? He'd helped her with English, and she'd introduced him to the lay of the land, so to speak. Why then did she look so angry, so ready to pounce and do some serious damage to his face?

"But no goodbye?" she shrilled again. "Who leaves with no *adeus*?" Her finger jabbed his way, and Easton had to force himself not to flinch. "A coward, that's who."

Coward? Whoa. That was hitting below the belt. Easton was no coward. He was more of an . . . avoider, a getter-out while the going's still good.

He wiped his palms across his soaked shorts, which did more harm than good. Like this conversation. "Samah, I don't like goodbyes. All the sadness and tears and . . . well, it isn't for me."

Her anger came back in a flash. "I would not cry for any man."

She could say that now because she was angry. Last night, however, after the long, passionate kiss they'd shared, tears would have been a sure thing. Easton would bet his beloved Manny Ramirez-signed baseball on it.

"What would you have done?" he asked.

"I would hug you and kiss you and say I would miss you and ask you to write. I would give you a . . . *adequado* goodbye."

Easton lifted an eyebrow. She seemed less mad now, more like her usual self. Maybe this didn't have to be as awkward as he thought. Maybe it could actually end on a good note.

He shifted in his seat. "Believe it or not I *am* going to miss you, Samah. We've had fun together, haven't we?"

She shook her head, her jaw still taut. "We had more than fun, *meu xodó.* I gave you some of my heart. My family took you in and fed you. We showed you our country and culture. And this is how you thank us? Thank *me?*"

As much as Easton hated goodbyes, he hated this more. The guilt. The reminder that he had, in a way, used Samah, just like he'd used many women along the way. He dated them for their knowledge of their homelands, for their beauty and spirit, and for the companionship they offered. Not once had Easton considered anything long-term with anyone. His Facebook, Twitter, blogging, and Instagram "friends" consisted of family, a few close friends, and readers. He didn't have time to stay in touch with everyone he met along the way. And what would be the point anyway?

"You're right, Samah," said Easton. "I should have said goodbye. I'm sorry."

Her palm flashed to his cheek and smacked him hard. He clenched his jaw to keep from cursing.

"You should be sorry," she said. "No, I would never cry for you, but I hope one day you give your heart to someone. To . . ." She groped for the right word. "How do you say: I give to you, you give to me?"

"Exchange?"

"*Si.*" She nodded. "To exchange hearts is beautiful and lovely. It makes you feel . . ." Her palms covered her heart as she searched for the words to explain, saying finally, "More than full. Bigger than yourself."

Easton nodded, pretending like he understood, like he knew what she was talking about. But he'd never felt that way about a woman before. Maybe it wasn't in his chemical makeup. He'd always considered his life both adventurous and fulfilling as is, but Samah made him wonder if he was missing out on something.

"And when it happens," added Samah, apparently not finished, "I hope she breaks your heart."

The passenger door opened and she swung out of the car. At some point during their conversation, the rain had let up and only a misty sprinkle remained. Mother Nature had always seemed to love Samah. Easton had the crazy feeling that if he got out of the car, the rain would rush down in torrents on him and him alone.

"*Adeus*, Easton Allard." The door slammed shut, and a fiery Portuguese woman with flawless skin and a good heart walked out of his life.

For the first time since he'd begun traveling, Easton felt a pang of something. Loss maybe? Dissatisfaction? Loneliness?

No. Easton wasn't dissatisfied with his life. He was alone when he chose to be and not alone when he didn't. He wasn't lonely. But as he watched the little blue car speed away, he felt something foreign, something that had more of a taste than a name.

Sour.

Squirming, Easton quickly turned the key and started the engine, feeling a sudden anxiousness. It was definitely time to go home.

chapter 2

About a month later

"Marry me."

Derek's warm breath tickled Lani's neck as the meaning of the words sent a scattering of goosebumps down her spine.

She gasped and drew back, eyes wide and mind whirling. She searched Derek's face, saw the hope in his blue eyes, the determination of his jaw, felt his earnestness in the tight way he held her. A fan of old Cary Grant movies, the day Lani had first met Derek Fulstrom in her freshman biology class at California State University, he'd reminded her of the actor. Tall, dark hair, chestnut eyes, the adorable way he shoved his hands in his pockets and ducked his head when he didn't know what to say. Even his approach to their relationship had been old-fashioned. They'd dated all through college, and he hadn't kissed her until the end of their junior year.

Derek was a rock—her rock. Nine years into their relationship and 2,500 miles later, his patience, support, and friendship never wavered. He'd always been a phone call, text message, or plane ticket away.

Right now he was a breath away.

Marry me. The words buzzed through Lani's mind like a current.

She continued to search his eyes, wondering how long he'd been thinking about this. Knowing the slow, methodical way he made decisions, probably a few years, and yet Lani felt blindsided. She'd thought this embrace, like all the others during the past five years, meant "See you in another six months" not "Marry me." But now that she thought about it, she probably should have seen the writing on the wall. During the past year, Derek had hinted more and more that he was ready for her to move back to her hometown of Carlsbad, where she'd be a mere forty miles away from where Derek now lived in Mission Viejo.

But Lani wasn't ready to move back. Hāna had become home, and the thought of leaving her grandmother made her chest clench.

"Derek, I . . ." Words failed her.

His hands moved from her waist to her upper arms, where they held her in a firm grip. "Your grandmother has been back on her feet for over two years. *Two years,* Lani. She will be okay on her own. How much longer are you going to put your life on hold for her?"

"She needs my help. She—"

Derek was shaking his head. "There are others who are happy to help. You know the people of this town are here for her, and Maaike has offered more than once to take over for you."

He was right. Puna didn't need her, not really. And yet every time Lani considered moving back, something tugged on her to stay. Actually, it was stronger than a tug. Her heart had rooted in Hāna and refused to budge.

For two years, Lani had been conjuring up excuses to remain in Hāna because she didn't want to leave. What would she do back in Carlsbad, anyway? Start her own bed and breakfast? Hardly. California was saturated with hotels, resorts, vacation rentals, and everything else. It would take a miracle to make something happen there, and Lani didn't believe in miracles.

The only lure that even tempted her back was Derek. Her two older brothers had long since married and moved away, and after her parents had split several years before, only her workaholic mother remained in Carlsbad. Her father, a popular motivational speaker, had been on the road since Lani could remember. The last she'd heard from him was a postcard from England for Christmas.

"Lani, it's time to come home," said Derek, pulling her attention back to him. "Please."

"I am home, Derek," she whispered.

But he didn't understand. The hurt in his expression conveyed that much. His hands fell from her arms, and his voice flattened. "I assumed 'home' would mean being with me."

"I didn't mean it like that," Lani said quickly. Hurting Derek was the last thing she wanted to do.

"How did you mean it then?"

"Only that Puna has taught me what family means, and Hāna has come to feel like home. My ties here have nothing to do with my feelings for you."

Derek sighed and shoved his hands in his pockets, his gaze moving toward the ocean where the sun was still rising. His plane would depart in a little over three hours, which meant he'd have to leave soon. But how could he drive away with so much still to say?

"What are your feelings for me?" he asked.

Lani blinked, wondering how to answer. He'd never been so blunt before. "I love you. You know that."

"*Why* do you love me?"

"Because you're good and kind and strong and my best friend. Because I care deeply about you."

"You could say the same thing about Puna. Or even Ahi."

Lani didn't understand. What did he want her to say? Wasn't that the definition of love?

"Why do you love *me*?" she asked, turning the question around.

His expression softened, and he tucked some of her long, dark hair behind her ear before his palms immediately framed her face, touching her tenderly. "You are the most beautiful woman I have ever known. Your face fills my thoughts every moment of the day. Your laughter makes me happier. Your smile makes me weak. Your touch makes me yearn for more. I admire the way you meet life head-on with optimism and grace, the way you packed your bags and flew across the ocean because a woman you knew only as a distant grandmother needed your help." He paused. "But now it's my turn, Lani. *I* need you. And I need to know if you need me too."

His words warmed her heart, and his confidence quieted her mind. "Yes," Lani breathed. Her feelings may not run as strong and deep as his did, but she loved him more now than she had five years ago. If she put her focus back where it belonged—on him—maybe in another year or two she'd catch up.

Derek was right. It was long past time for him to become her home.

"Give me a few weeks to say my goodbyes and tie up some loose ends, and I'll move back to California." She couldn't bring herself to say the word "home" just yet.

Derek's lips lifted into a contagious smile, and he pulled her tight against him, kissing her with passion and the promise of a bright future. "As soon as you get home," he murmured against her lips, "we'll go ring shopping and make it official. Okay?"

"Sounds great." Lani's spirits lifted as the glow of his happiness embraced them both. He laughed. She laughed. He smiled, and so did she. For a moment, everything felt right.

But as she waved goodbye and watched the silver Focus disappear through the dense green foliage of eastern Maui, the sunny warmth was pushed aside by a cool breeze that chilled her from the inside out.

Lani shook off the feeling as she wandered back inside to get a start on the day's work. At her desk, she clasped her fingers behind her and arched her back, giving it a good stretch before she took a seat. Lani only had thirty minutes until breakfast preparations would begin, and she needed to make the most of that time.

Now where was that stack of invoices? She began shuffling papers around, trying to find them, when someone cleared her throat not far away.

Lani glanced up in surprise. A striking and petite Asian woman stood before her wearing a floral shirt and mint-green slacks. Her hair was pulled back in a bun at the nape of her head, and light from the window caught the sheen on a lovely, pearl-studded comb.

Where had the woman come from? Lani had been outside only moments before. There had been no new cars in the drive, and the bell on the door hadn't rung. How long had she been waiting? And who was she? New guests weren't scheduled to arrive until the weekend.

"I'm so sorry," Lani said, standing to find she was over a

head taller than the woman. "I didn't see you there. May I help you?"

The woman nodded politely. "I'm here to check in. My reservation is under the name Pearl." She had a Chinese accent.

Lani's brow furrowed. *Check in?* No one by the name of Pearl was listed on the reservation list—at least not anytime during the next three weeks. Lani knew because she'd gone over them only yesterday. "I'm sorry, but you must have us confused with another bed and breakfast. We're booked out the entire summer."

Pearl squinted at a paper in her hand. "Is this not Halemahina Pumehana?" Even with her mild accent, she'd pronounced the name perfectly. Most guests tried, but failed—some by a little, others, a lot. It had even taken Lani a few weeks to get the name down. Pearl, on the other hand, seemed to know exactly where she was.

"May I see that?" Lani nodded at the paper Pearl held.

"Of course." She handed it to Lani.

One look, and Lani panicked. It was a printout of a reservation booked online through their website with a check-in date of today for the Akua room. How had this happened? Mr. and Mrs. Porter had reserved the room months ago and would be here two more nights. And Dr. Jenkins and her daughter were in the Hema room until Monday. Lani had corresponded with both guests prior to them coming. She'd sent directions, checked them in on arrival, and offered suggestions for activities.

She'd never so much as seen Pearl's name before.

Lani had no idea what to say or do. "Oh my goodness, I am so sorry, but—"

The bell on the door jingled, and Mr. and Mrs. Porter breezed into the lobby, carrying their suitcases.

"Oh, Lani. Good, you're here," said Mrs. Porter in her sugary sweet voice as she peered at Lani beneath the brim of a giant, white sunhat. "You've been such a dear to us, but Ray and I decided last night that Hāna is much too quiet for us." She threw her arms out to the side in a dramatic gesture. "We need parties, excursions, shows, luaus on the beach, and . . . well, a few more people than Hāna has to offer."

"Don't forget massages," added her husband.

Mrs. Porter tittered a laugh. "Yes, definitely massages. Anyway, I do hate to spring this on you, but we're off to Lahaina this morning for what we hope is a grand adventure. Thank you for being so hospitable. This place is just charming. We'll be sure to tell all our friends about it and leave raving reviews on TripAdvisor. Feel free to charge our credit card for the remaining rent since we are cutting out early."

"What about breakfast?" asked Lani as she accepted Mr. Porter's credit card and scrambled to get the paperwork together.

"No need to worry about feeding us, my dear. We enjoyed the last of the loaf of yummy banana bread you left for us yesterday."

"Are you sure?" said Lani, handing them the receipt.

"Positive," said Mrs. Porter. "Really, you've been lovely."

In a flurry of suitcases and bells, they waved goodbye with an "Aloha" and were off.

"Aloha," Lani said belatedly. She looked from the door to Pearl before coming to her senses. "It looks as though a room just opened up. It's available until Friday morning. Will three days work for you?"

Pearl slid the reservation printout back into her handbag before Lani had a chance to see the checkout date.

She nodded and smiled, as though this sort of coincidence happened every day. "That will do nicely for now. Mahalo."

For now? Lani thought as she fished the rental contract from the drawer. "You can look this over on the lanai, if you'd like, while I make you some fresh—"

"Hot chocolate?" Pearl's expression brightened. "I do love a good hot chocolate."

Lani nodded. She had been about to say juice, but they had hot chocolate as well—she hoped. "Okay then. One hot chocolate it is. I'll also need about an hour to get your room ready, if that's okay."

"Of course. I'll wait on the lanai." Pearl offered Lani a serene smile, dipped her head, and walked outside. This time the bells on the door jingled the way they always did.

Lani was staring at the closed door, trying to make sense of what had just happened, when Puna waltzed in wearing a turquoise and orange muumuu.

"Cheer up, *pilialoha*," said her grandmother. "Derek will be back soon. He always comes back."

Lani blinked, wondering what her grandmother was talking about. And like a bad aftertaste, the memory of that morning came back. Derek. Proposal. California.

Lani slowly sank down in the chair and looked at the woman who'd become more dear to her than her own mother. Short, gray curls surrounded her slightly wrinkled, age-spotted face, always looking neat despite the humidity. It was going to break Lani's heart to leave.

"Puna, there's something I need to tell you."

The task chair squeaked as Lani adjusted positions and prodded herself a little closer to the computer while she

14

waited for the painfully slow site to load. She'd tried to talk her grandmother into upgrading to high-speed, satellite internet, but her grandmother had always said that what their guests really needed was to get out of tune with the internet and more in tune with nature.

Lani never bothered to remind her that it was because of the internet that their two rooms booked out well in advance, and a high-speed connection would make their work so much more efficient. It would especially come in handy now, when shopping for flights could easily take the entire two weeks Lani had left.

"When do you leave again?" Her grandmother's sweet, airy voice sounded from behind.

Lani smiled, knowing her grandmother knew exactly when she'd be leaving. This was her way of bringing up the conversation again now that she'd had time to plan a counter-attack.

"Fourteen days," said Lani.

"Only two weeks?" Her grandmother tried to sound properly surprised, but failed. "But you only just got here."

Lani's lips lifted into a soft smile as she scrolled through a list of possible flights. "I've been here five years, Puna."

"Yes, that's what I'm saying. Only five years—not nearly enough time for Hāna to seep into your soul the way it should." Her grandmother pulled an armchair forward and planted her slightly plump frame at Lani's side.

The page finally loaded, and Lani grimaced at the amount the airline was asking for a one-way ticket. Maybe she'd been too hasty in saying she'd move in two weeks. Last-minute airfare was the equivalent of highway robbery.

"Trust me," Lani said. "Hāna has done more than enough seeping into my soul. It's time for Derek to do some seeping."

"Derek sch-merek." Her grandmother waved a dismissive hand.

Lani paused in her search long enough to shoot her grandmother a look of confusion. "I thought you liked Derek."

"Oh, I do." Her tight, gray curls bobbed up and down as she nodded. "And so do you."

Lani joined in the nodding. "Which is why I need to go. I need to show him exactly how much I like him."

"But not love?" Her grandma lifted a wrinkly brow.

Lani rolled her eyes. "Love. I meant love."

"No, you didn't."

"Puna, don't start with me. Derek has waited long enough, and I've made my decision. It's time for me to move back to California."

Her grandmother's eyes became merry as she tapped two fingers against Lani's wrist. "See? You keep making my point for me. I wish you could hear yourself."

"I think *you're* the one who's having trouble hearing."

"If you were truly in love," continued her grandmother, "there would be no decision to make. You would have flown home two years ago."

Lani's fingers stilled on the keyboard. From the moment she'd waved goodbye to Derek that morning, she'd become a robot, forming lists and checking off items. She knew if she stopped to think about leaving—*really* think about it— uncomfortable things would happen. Lumps would form in her throat, her stomach would knot, and her heart shrivel.

She'd rushed through her morning routine, trying not to smell the white plumeria that she arranged in a vase for Pearl's lanai, attempting to ignore the undulations of the Koa flooring in the kitchen as she prepared Hawaiian omelets for Pearl and the Jenkins. In the lobby, she'd purposely avoided looking at her favorite picture of her and her grandmother, grinning in front of Waimoku Falls. Puna had insisted on hiking the Pipiwai trail as soon as her physical therapy ended. She'd said she needed proof that her new knees would be better than the old ones, and nothing would stop her. It had been a long and slow journey, and by the end of it Puna had been wobbly and sore, but she'd made it. Lani had never been more proud of her grandmother.

Memories. They hung from every wall, stretched across every floor, shone from every window, and mingled with every breath. Only Lani's to-do lists kept them at a distance.

But now, with Puna sitting at her side, smelling like coconut and wearing her favorite muumuu, it was impossible to continue with robot-mode.

"I don't want to leave, Puna," said Lani quietly. "I'm going to miss you so much. I can't stand thinking about it. But I can't let Derek wait for me any longer. It's not fair to him."

"I agree." Her grandmother's head bobbed up and down as though she really did.

"You do?"

"Yes. Derek definitely shouldn't wait any longer. He should move on to someone else."

Lani sighed and shook her head. "And where would that leave me? Should I stay here and marry Ahe? Or better yet, Taavatti?"

"Heaven's no," said her grandmother. "Taavatti is twice your age, child. And Ahe, while a dear, could never stand up to you. You need a man who's as strong-minded as you. Someone who challenges your views, makes you change some of them and keeps you holding fast to others. Someone who makes your heart soar."

Lani's thoughts went to Derek, and she frowned. "You make it sound like a romance novel."

"As it should be."

"No, Puna. Romance novels are fiction. My life is real. Derek is loyal, good, and kind. He's . . . a rock." Lani had meant it as a compliment, but it sounded so staid and unromantic, so she quickly added, "My rock."

That didn't sound much better.

"Rocks are for sitting, dear. And stubbing your toes. When it comes to soaring, they only weigh you down."

Lani shrugged. "Maybe I don't want to soar."

"If you knew what it felt like, you would."

Lani thought of her parents' relationship and how her mother had once said that her father had swept her off her feet only to drop her with a bruising thud ten years and two kids later. If there was one thing nine years of dating had done for Lani, it had assured her that Derek would never drop her. In her mind, rock-solid loyalty beat soaring any day.

"Derek's qualities are important to me. And if I don't go now, I'll lose him, and I can honestly say I don't want that to happen. He's become very dear to me."

Her grandmother clasped her fingers on her lap and studied Lani for a moment. "Can we at least make a compromise?"

Lani hesitated. "What sort of compromise?"

"Well, this is all happening a little fast for me. I've gotten used to having you around and relying on you too much. Would you be willing to stay through the summer? Three months instead of two weeks? It's our busiest season, and I could use your help one last summer. You can teach me all you know about computers, and I can come to terms with losing you. Besides that"—she nodded toward the computer—"airplane tickets will probably be cheaper in the fall."

All three very good points. And as Lani considered her grandmother's compromise, a heaviness lifted from her shoulders. Three months would also give Lani some time to get used to the idea of leaving. It all fell into place like a happy win-win.

Until she thought of Derek. Would he be willing to give her three more months?

Probably. He wouldn't like it, but he would. Which was exactly why Lani refused to let him go. Men like Derek Lundstrum were about as rare as seeing the elusive Hawaiian Blue butterfly. In the five years Lani had lived in Hāna, she'd never seen one, and unless a miracle happened, she probably never would.

Another lump in her throat and twist of her stomach.

She really needed to keep her thoughts on Derek and away from Maui, her grandmother, and everything else she'd come to love during the past five years.

"Okay, Puna. Let me talk to Derek first, and we'll see. But if I do stay, when September comes, I need you to let me go without a fight. Deal?"

Her grandmother's expression brightened, and a happy smile formed. "If you still want to go, I promise to let you."

Lani gave her grandmother a look of amused tolerance.

"In the meantime—" Puna pushed her chair back and stood. "We have work to do. You know that little house on the hill? We need to get it aired out and cleaned up."

"Why?"

"Because I've rented it out for the summer," said her grandmother as she breezed out of the room.

Lani stared at the open doorway as she tried to process the news. The little house on the hill? The one overrun with blue jade vines and white shrimp plants? The home of several geckos, spiders, and bugs? The home Lani hadn't set foot in since she arrived because it was off limits?

Airplane tickets forgotten, Lani leapt from her chair and skidded into the hall as she raced after her grandmother. "Puna!"

chapter 3

E aston raised his sunglasses to the crown of his head and pulled the strap of his laptop bag tighter over his shoulder while his eyes adjusted to the dim light in the lobby. A floor-to-ceiling window stood behind him, but the overcast skies and gargantuan Koa tree in the yard out front enshrouded the space with a heavy shade. The room smelled like a mixture of pina colada and aged, humidified wood and looked exactly the way it had been described on the website.

A painted picture of a Hawaiian coastline hung from the wall in front of him, and he stepped forward, wishing he could be here on vacation instead of for work. When it came to his "job," Maui was the last place he wanted to be.

A woman with long, almost-black hair sat at a desk, hunched over some paperwork. Apparently, she was immersed in whatever she was doing because she didn't acknowledge him even though the bells on the door should have alerted her to his presence.

And yet . . .

Nothing.

Easton was about to clear his throat when she finally spoke. "The stare-me-down challenge isn't going to work, Puna. I refuse to forgive you until my body stops aching and you explain to me why you suddenly felt the need to—" She looked up, and the rest of her words died a quick death.

Her dark brown, slightly wide-set eyes—the kind a guy could drown in—widened. With long eyelashes, eyebrows arched at the most intriguing spot, deeply tanned oval face, high cheekbones, and lips the soft pink of the flowers he'd passed on his way in, the woman was flat-out gorgeous.

Easton found himself not minding at all that she'd made him wait.

She quickly stood and smoothed down the floral skirt she wore before her gaze returned to his. Only three or four inches shorter than his six-foot frame, she was slender and curved in all the right places. A slight blush darkened her cheeks as she took him in, and Easton hid his smile. He was used to turning women's heads and had long since gotten over any self-consciousness that came from it.

She finally found her voice. "I'm sorry. You're obviously not Puna."

"No, thank goodness." He grinned. "Sounds to me like she's on your blacklist, and I'd rather not start off that way." He stepped forward and held out a hand. "Easton Allard. I spoke to a Cora Kahele on the phone last week about renting a private bungalow?"

A look of surprise replaced the blush. "*You're* Easton Allard?" This time she looked at him—not as a woman appreciating an attractive man, but as a woman trying to solve a riddle.

"Last time I checked," said Easton. Apparently, he had a reputation already. And from the way her brows furrowed, it couldn't be that great of one. If he didn't know any better, he would think Samah had somehow called ahead to warn her. He smiled in a way that usually made women smile back, but those soft pink lips didn't budge.

"I'm glad you're finally here," she said. Her tone wasn't annoyed or rude, just . . . curious. "I've been wanting to ask you how in the world you convinced my grandmother to rent that shack to you for the summer."

Now Easton was confused. He'd been told it was a cozy bungalow set on a hill with three-hundred-and-sixty-degree views of the most gorgeous countryside on Maui, along with views of the ocean.

"Shack?" he repeated.

"Oh, sorry. I meant"—her fingers made quote marks in the air—"'bungalow.'"

"Am I . . . missing something?" If the woman hadn't recognized his name, Easton would have thought he'd come to the wrong place, but . . . she *had* recognized his name and seemed to think he knew something he didn't.

She completely ignored his question. She planted her hands on the desk and leaned forward. "Seriously, how do you know my grandmother? In the five years I've been here, she's refused to talk about the shack, set foot in the place, or even tackle the landscape around it. Every time I ask, all I get is 'Leave it alone. That's what I do.' Like it's some haunted shrine that will bring bad luck to anyone who looks at it. Then out of the blue you call, and suddenly it's okay to enter the premises. Why is that?"

She looked at Easton expectantly, as though he could offer an explanation, which he couldn't. For all he knew, her grandmother had gone senile, though she'd sounded perfectly lucid over the phone. The laptop bag was beginning to dig into his shoulder, so Easton set it on a nearby chair. "I have no clue what you're talking about. I've never met your grandmother before. I just did a quick internet search of places to stay near Hāna and saw that your bed and breakfast got stellar reviews. So I crossed my fingers that you'd have an opening and called. Cora asked a few questions and told me that I was in luck. That you had a"—this time, it was Easton making the quotes—"'newly renovated bungalow' available for the entire summer. So I booked it and here I am."

Her eyes narrowed slightly, as though she didn't believe his story. "The entire summer is a long time."

"Yes, it is."

"Mind if I ask if you're here for work or fun?"

"Both" was the only explanation he offered. Over the years, Easton had become a pro at evading personal questions. It was rarely in his best interest to reveal too much about himself, and Hawaii was the last place he would ever want to come clean. And besides, his work *was* typically enjoyable.

Before she could ask any more personal questions, he diverted the conversation back to where it had been headed before. "So about this 'bungalow' I've rented that is really an overgrown, run-down shack that hasn't been lived-in for who knows how long."

"Well, *now* it's not," she said, defending the place she'd only just disparaged. "Like my grandmother told you over the phone, it's been . . . renovated." She sighed and took a seat in her task chair, swiping her long, wavy hair to the side of her face. Easton couldn't stop looking at her eyes. Over fifty-five percent of the world's population had brown eyes, and yet hers seemed different somehow. Rich and expressive, yet warm and mysterious.

Easton pulled a chair forward and took a seat across from her. He didn't usually have a conversation like this on

24

check-in. It was . . . intriguing. This place was intriguing. The woman was intriguing. He wanted to know more.

"Do you have a name?" he blurted.

She studied him a moment before nodding. "Lokelani Whitman. And I apologize for the, uh . . . unconventional greeting. I don't usually make guests go through a Q&A before checking them in. I just don't understand my grandmother and was hoping you could give me some clues."

"Wish I could," he said. "What did you say your name was? Loke-a-what?" She'd spoken so fast, he hadn't caught her entire name.

"Lok-e-*lani*," she said slower, emphasizing the last two syllables.

A Hawaiian name, and yet she didn't appear like she had much Hawaiian blood in her. Slightly tanner skin and wider eyes, maybe, but other than that, she looked as much like a mainlander as him. Yes, she definitely intrigued him.

"I like it," said Easton, "But four syllables makes it a mouthful. Do you have a nickname?"

"My friends call me Lani."

Easton nodded, thinking the name fit her well. "It's good to meet you, Lani."

"I said my *friends* call me that." Her expression contained humor and a challenge all rolled into one. She was teasing him.

He chuckled. "Considering I'm a friendly guy, I'm hopeful I'll be able to call you that sooner than later. Like you said, summer is a long time."

"Just don't get too friendly," she said as she sifted through papers. "I'm already taken."

Taken. Easton's smile became pasted. He glanced at her ring finger, and when he saw nothing there, quirked an eyebrow. "You sure about that?"

"His name is Derek Lundstrum. And the ring is coming."

Easton tried to hide his disappointment with humor. "Coming? As in . . . in the mail? Are you a mail-order bride?"

"No." Lani opened a file drawer and pulled out some paperwork and a pen. She held them out to him. "Mind looking this over and signing it for me? It's our rental agreement."

He took them and quickly scrawled his name across the bottom, not bothering to read any of it. The elusive ring was much more interesting. "Boat then?"

"No. I'm going to need a deposit. How would you like to pay for it?"

Easton fished his wallet from his pocket and handed her a credit card. "Carrier pigeons?"

That elicited a laugh—a lovely laugh—along with a shake of her head and a credit card swipe. "No, though that would be really cool."

"Airplane?"

She handed his card back. "That's probably as close as you're going to get, so sure, let's go with airplane."

He shoved the card into his wallet and pocketed it, his eyes never leaving hers. "So a plane-ordered bride then."

"I don't take orders from anyone or anything."

"Except paying guests?"

"*Even* paying guests," she said. "But feel free to make as many *requests* as you'd like." She fished a key from a drawer and walked around the side of the desk, her hips swaying and her floral, knee-length skirt swishing as she walked past him. "If you'd care to come with me, I'll show you to your newly renovated bungalow."

Lani's hand shook a little as she tried to turn the key in the lock. It resisted, so she gave it a jiggle and tried again. Not even a budge. What in the world? It had slid right in the few times before when she'd locked or unlocked the door.

Stupid, sticky lock. Go in.

"You sure you have the right key?" Easton's smooth, distinctive voice sounded behind her. He could easily be a voice-double for Chris Pine. She could listen to him talk all day—and look at him too. Tall, but not too tall, defined shoulders, light green eyes, and dark blond hair that was shorter on the sides and swept up like a churning sea on top.

Lani forced her mind back to the lock. *Why won't you open?* She needed to get away from Easton and his voice and the way he made her stomach feel like she was riding in a boat during a storm. Not seasickness, but not okay either.

"Yes, I'm sure," said Lani, pulling it from the lock. "See?" She pointed at the plastic keychain where the word "bungalow" had been written.

Easton shrugged. "You did say it was haunted. Maybe a bunch of Hawaiian spirits are trying to keep a haole like me out."

Ignoring the comment, she shoved the key back in and jiggled it harder. When it still wouldn't turn, Lani sighed in frustration, blowing some of her hair from her face. She looked back at Easton, who was now leaning against the railing of the lanai, folding his arms and watching her with amusement.

"How do you feel about climbing through windows?" she asked him.

His eyebrow lifted and his lips quirked. "I try not to make a habit of it." Pushing away from the railing, he nodded toward the door. "Mind if I give it a try?"

Lani shrugged and stepped to the side. "Feel free. But if

the Hawaiian spirits didn't let me open it, I doubt they'll let you."

His shoulder brushed hers, causing a breakout of goosebumps on her arm, so Lani stepped farther away. Not only did he have his good looks going for him, but he was confident and suave in a way that most people couldn't pull off. She squirmed, wishing she could walk away and leave him to it.

Easton tried the lock, failed, then took the key out to examine it before trying again. "I really don't think this key fits."

"It does," she insisted. "It's worked every other time. Trust me."

He chuckled, and the sound made Lani's heart flutter. She took another step away. What was going on with her? She'd been around handsome men before without this strong of a reaction. It had to be the mystery surrounding his arrival—surrounding him. Who was he, and why did Puna suddenly want to open this place *for* him? Nothing was adding up or making sense.

"I take it this wasn't part of your renovation?" Giving up, he pulled the key from the lock and handed it back before walking across the lanai and planting his palms on the railing. He scanned the property and nodded at the hammock nestled between two jacaranda trees. "I suppose I could sleep there."

At least he was taking this all in stride. Lani had to give him credit for that. Most guests would have fled to the Hāna Hotel by now. She tried the key one more time before giving up. "There's an open window around the side. If you don't mind hopping through it, you can sleep on a, uh . . . semi-comfortable bed tonight."

"I don't hop, and *semi-comfortable* bed?" He snickered.

"I'm thinking your grandmother should handle all marketing from here on out. You're not so great at it."

She chose to ignore the last part of his comment. "Scooting is a better word," she said. "All you have to do is scoot through a window."

"Why don't I help *you* scoot through it?" His lips lifted into a half smile that made her heart flutter again.

"If I wasn't wearing a skirt, I would."

Easton chuckled again as though he couldn't believe this was happening to him. "Okay, fine. I'll do the scooting. On one condition."

"Okay. Fine," said Lani, anticipating his condition. "I'll give you a discount on your room, although the rate Puna quoted you is already half the price of our other rentals."

"Your other rentals aren't haunted," he pointed out.

"They haven't been newly renovated either."

Easton laughed. "Actually, my condition has nothing to do with my room rate and more to do with you."

The flirtatious way he looked at her made her eyes narrow. "I told you. I'm taken."

"My, you're presumptuous. That's not what I was thinking either."

"Then what?" Lani was beginning to lose patience. She had other things to do, other things to think about, and another man to call.

Easton came to stand in front of her and leaned a shoulder against the peeling green paint on the side of the bungalow. That was one of the many things Lani hadn't had time to do—scrape and repaint.

"Well?" she asked when he continued to stand there.

"I was just thinking," he said slowly, "that only a *friend* could get away with asking me to 'scoot' through a window, so . . . *Lani,* is it?"

Spoken with that voice, and in that low, flirtatious way, her name sounded wonderful. Wow, he was hard to resist. She swallowed and looked away in an attempt to calm her racing heart. She would need to keep her distance if she was going to keep her head focused where it needed to be—on Derek Lundstrom, the man she was practically engaged to marry.

Out of desperation or self-preservation—she couldn't decide which—she agreed. "Fine. If Lokelani is too hard for you to say, feel free to call me Lani. Now c'mon, I'll show you where the window is."

She trotted down the steps and walked around the side of the house, pointing at a small, opened window above her head as she walked past. "There it is. I'll go find something for you to stand on."

"I think 'hopping' was a more accurate word."

Lani tried not to laugh as she walked around to the back of the house and grabbed a metal garbage can. She hauled it back to where Easton stood and turned it upside down. "There you go."

He eyed the over-turned can with skepticism. "This is a very unconventional way to get inside my room."

"Something tells me you're a fan of the unconventional."

"Will I have to do this every time I come and go?"

"Not if you leave your door unlocked."

He bit his lower lip, trying not to smile, then hopped up on the can, grabbed the top of the window, and gracefully swung his legs and body through the opening. A moment later, his head peered down at her. "Thank you for the aloha welcome to Hāna, *Lani*. It's been an adventure."

She dropped to a curtsy and nodded. "If there's anything you need, please don't hesitate to ask."

"Oh, you can count on it." With a wink, his handsome face disappeared inside the room.

Lani let out a breath of relief as she sauntered back down the grassy slope toward the main house, where she and Puna lived and cooked and worked. Not far to the side was a smaller cottage, where the Akua and Hema rooms were located. Lani looked over the property, appreciating its beauty for the thousandth time, and tried not to think of having to leave it all behind in only a few months' time.

Derek, as expected, had been the perfect gentleman, agreeing that it would be better for Lani to stay one last busy season and take the time to train her replacement. But every time Lani had pulled out her phone to call Maaike, her fingers froze, her heart stopped, and she couldn't do it. Not yet, anyway. In time, she would have no choice, but she still had the entire summer before her. Two weeks was really all she would need to train Maaike.

"Aloha, Lani," called out Pearl from her lanai, lifting her hand in greeting.

Lani changed directions and headed over. Pearl, who didn't seem to have a last name—not even on the check she'd written as a deposit—was another mystery. Originally, she was supposed to leave the end of last week, but the Gettys had something come up unexpectedly and couldn't make it, so Pearl had opted to stay until the following Wednesday, when another guest would be arriving. Lani wasn't sure what the woman did all day or why she desired to stay. She seemed to enjoy chatting with Puna, learning about all the flowers and plants, strolling around the property, and relaxing on the lanai. She was rarely indoors.

"Aloha, Pearl," said Lani. "Are you enjoying your day?"

Pearl nodded toward the shack/bungalow on the hill. "I see you have a new visitor. From this distance, he looks very handsome."

"He is handsome," answered Lani honestly. "And apparently, he'll be here until the end of August."

"Ah, so you'll have time to really get to know him." The way Pearl gazed at Lani made it feel like she could see into her soul. "It must be hard sometimes, always saying aloha-hello then aloha-goodbye a few days later. You never get to know people as who they really are."

Lani had never really thought about it before—at least not to the point where she considered it hard to do. In the past there had been a few guests that Lani had been sad to see go, but it was part of the job. Not everyone could stay in Hāna long-term like she had been able to do.

"Oh, I don't mind," said Lani. "I have Puna, and I've made some good friends here in Hāna. I enjoy visiting with each guest that comes to stay, and I try my hardest to see that they have a wonderful time. I've never really felt like I'm missing out on anything."

Pearl nodded slowly, considering Lani's words. "Will Rogers once said, 'A stranger is just a friend I haven't met yet.' Isn't that a beautiful way to look at it?"

Lani agreed. It was. But the way Pearl looked at her, with one eyebrow lifted expectantly, gave Lani the impression that the older woman was trying to tell her something. But why? Lani had always made friends with each and every guest—or at least, as good of friends as one could make in only a few days' time. Was Pearl implying she should make more of an effort?

"The new guest," Pearl continued. "What's his name?"

"Easton Allard."

"And what is his purpose, coming to Hāna for the summer?"

Lani's gaze drifted back up the rise to the little bungalow on the hill. "I don't know," she said. "He was very evasive."

Pearl nodded again, as though she'd already known that. "You know, Lani. I've been around for a long time and have met a lot of people in my travels. I've come to discover that those with the hardest shells tend to have the softest hearts."

Easton? A soft heart? Lani almost laughed at the thought. A hard shell, probably. But soft heart? That was doubtful. No, there were some definite holes in that theory. Derek, for example, had a soft shell *and* a soft heart, and Puna—well, she had the softest heart of them all.

"I guess I'll have to take your word for it," said Lani, taking a step back. "I hope you enjoy the rest of your day, Pearl."

"I always do," she answered. Then she lifted her hand into the air, and Lani got a glimpse of a butterfly resting on her finger before it fluttered its wings and flew away.

Jaw dropping, Lani stared in awe. "Was that—?" No, that couldn't have been a Hawaiian Blue. They were too rare.

"A butterfly? Yes," answered Pearl. "The little darling landed on my hand earlier and has been keeping me company this morning. I'm sorry to see it go."

Lani blinked, feeling like at some point during the past week she'd fallen down a rabbit hole and landed in a very strange world. And it had all begun the day she'd looked up from her desk to find Pearl standing in the lobby.

chapter 4

"**P**una, what aren't you telling me?" Lani asked as she basted olive oil across two small tuna steaks. Puna liked to eat dinner earlier, around five, and be in bed by eight. Running a bed and breakfast was hard work, and Lani had no idea how her grandmother kept at it day after day. And when she wasn't busy with guests and the property, her grandmother would visit friends and neighbors, making sure everyone was okay and in good spirits.

"I always tell you everything," said her grandmother.

"No," said Lani, sprinkling salt and pepper on the fish. "You always *dance* around everything."

"I don't know what you mean."

Lani sighed in frustration. She stepped out the door to the lanai and slid the steaks on the grill. Then she returned to the kitchen, folded her arms, and zeroed in on her grandmother. "Why was the shack off limits until last week?"

Puna continued chopping a mango. "The timing wasn't right."

"What's made it right now?"

Her grandmother tossed a pile of mango chunks into a bowl and smoothed her hands down the front of her blue and purple floral apron. "Pearl made a comment about how it was a shame that such a beautiful spot wasn't being put to good use. Not long after, a young man called who needed a place to stay for the summer. So I offered him the bungalow."

That still didn't answer the question. Lani tried to keep her frustration in check. "For the last five years I have been telling you the same thing—that you could increase your profits by fixing up and renting out the place, but you never once listened to me. Then a guest makes one comment, someone else calls, and suddenly it's a great idea?"

"Like I said, timing. A young man in need of a place to stay never called right after you suggested it. But when it happened after Pearl said something, I figured it was meant to be."

"Meant to be?" Puna always had her eccentricities, but this was a bit much, even for her. "The only reason it's suddenly 'meant to be' is because you made it that way. Easton's calling when he did was a lucky coincidence on his part."

Puna scooped up the mango skins and threw them in the garbage. As she passed Lani on her way to the fridge, she paused to pat her granddaughter's cheek. "Oh, *kealoha*, when are you going to learn that there are few happenstances in life? Most things occur for a reason. It's our job to figure that reason out."

Lani clamped her lips closed to keep from scoffing. "Puna, you know I love you, but I really think that all you're doing is letting Easton Allard take advantage of you. The rate he talked you down to is . . ." Lani searched her mind for a kind way of saying laughable.

"He didn't talk me down. He talked me up."

"What?" Lani stared at her grandmother.

"I offered him the bungalow for free, but he wouldn't hear of it."

Lani suddenly felt as though a strong conviction had been proven wrong, and it unsettled her. She'd assumed, all along, that Easton Allard had schmoozed his way to the low rental amount, when in reality, he'd done the reverse—which wouldn't have been the easiest thing to do. Lani knew from experience how stubborn her grandmother could be.

"So you're telling me that—"

"Sorry to interrupt," came Easton's voice from the open back door, "but there's a lot of smoke coming from the grill out here."

Oh no, the steaks! Lani sprinted forward, squeezed past Easton, and threw open the grill. She grabbed the spatula and quickly flipped the fish over, revealing a completely charred underside. Honestly, couldn't anything go right today?

"They look the way they smell," said Easton's voice near her ear.

Lani glanced over her shoulder and nearly whacked her face against his. Heat ran through her body that had nothing to do with the grill, and she side-stepped away—annoyed by him, by the burned fish, and by the whole world at the moment.

"Thanks for pointing that out. I didn't notice."

Puna poked her head out the door. "Oh, Lani. Did you burn the steaks again?"

Again? In the five years Lani had lived in Hāna, she'd only burned tuna steaks once—and only because she'd never cooked them before. Her grandmother made it sound like it was a daily occurrence.

"You burn fish often?" asked Easton.

"No," said Lani, shooting her grandmother a look that said, *Since you're the one who made him think that, you set him straight.*

Puna ignored "the look" and held out her hand. "You must be Easton. It's wonderful to meet you in person."

Easton accepted her hand with two of his, sandwiching her fingers between his like they were old friends. "You must be Cora. I'd recognize your voice anywhere."

Her grandmother actually blushed—*blushed!* It was like Easton had read a book called *How to Make People Fall in Love With You in Sixty Seconds or Less*—not that Lani had fallen under his spell. She mentally revised the title to read: *How To Make* Most *People Fall in Love With You . . .*

"Do you like the bungalow?" Puna asked warmly.

"It's just as you promised—charming, cozy, and definitely the best location on the island. In fact, this morning I had the most beautiful view right outside the bathroom window." He winked at Lani, and her cheeks grew warm. She blamed it on the hot grill and quickly turned off the heat.

"Lani, before I forget, I have a present for you." Easton went fishing in his pocket for something.

"Uh . . . it's way too soon for presents, isn't it?" Lani immediately clamped her mouth shut. Had she really just implied that there would come a time when it *wasn't* too soon? Good grief. What she needed to do was go straight to her room, pull the covers over her head, and not come out until her brain returned.

Easton held up a shiny, silver key that caught the light of the sun as it dangled from his fingers. Lani tried to read what was inscribed on the key chain when his other hand—a very smooth and warm hand—captured hers, holding it steady as he dropped the key onto her palm.

She stared at it, trying not to be affected by his touch but failing miserably. "What's this?" Attached to the key was a shiny, silver oval with an inscription that read, *The Bungalow.*

His touch left abruptly as his hand released hers. "Let's just say the lock problem has been resolved. That's your copy."

She looked from the key to him. "You replaced the lock?"

"I did."

"Where did you get one in Hāna?"

"Not at the general store, that's for sure."

"Then where?"

"Haiku."

Lani's jaw fell open for a moment before she closed it again. Haiku was an hour and a half drive down the famed Hāna Highway—the busiest, windiest road Lani had ever driven. Sure, the scenery was breathtaking, but you don't see much of it when you're the driver, and besides, the view from her lanai was also breathtaking. Lani hated the highway so much she only made the trip when absolutely necessary—usually about once a month—and only because there was a Costco in Kahului.

"You drove all the way to Haiku?"

"It's a beautiful drive."

"It's a horrible drive!" As he well knew because he'd already driven the road to get here. She quickly did the math in her head. Ouch.

"Well, a guy's got to be able to get in and out of his bungalow, doesn't he?"

A feeling of remorse elbowed Lani's stomach. She should have offered to get the lock fixed this morning. She should have driven to Haiku herself. She should have—

"I take it you're planning to burn the other side of that fish so they match?" He nodded toward the steaks, and Lani grabbed the spatula and immediately removed the charred tuna from the grill, slapping them down on the plate. They looked pitiful—all broken, cracked, and black. Proof that she was easily distracted.

"Maybe if you shred them and put the meat in a salad you won't taste the charcoal flavor," Easton offered.

Trying not to wince, Lani picked up the plate and dumped the fish into a nearby trashcan.

Easton stood over the can, shaking his head. "I feel like we should have a moment of silence. Tuna is some of my favorite fish, and well . . . it's kind of sad to see it go to waste. Would you like to say a few words, Lani?"

No, she didn't want to say a few words—to the fish or to Easton. She wanted him to walk back up the hill, shut himself in the bungalow with that new lock, and keep out of sight. Maybe then she'd be able to think clearly.

Instead, she muttered, "May they rest in peace."

Both Easton and Puna laughed.

"That was good of you to replace your own locks," said Puna, still standing in the kitchen doorway, looking much too delighted by their exchange. "Let us know the cost, along with what you spent for gas, and we'll take that off your rent."

"Please don't." There was no hint of schmooze in Easton's voice this time. He sounded completely sincere. "It was the least I could do. And believe it or not, I enjoy fixing things."

Lani glanced down to see the shiny, silver key resting in her hand, reminding her that she was in Easton's debt. She gulped down her pride, guilt, and discomfort in a painful swallow. "Yes, mahalo." Her voice sounded even more pitiful than the fish had looked.

"What was that?" Easton tipped his head in her direction, wearing a grin that told her he'd heard every word she'd said.

Get over yourself and thank the man, Lani told herself firmly. So she lifted her chin and reminded herself that he'd just taken three hours of his time to do something for her.

She met his gaze. "I said *mahalo.* I really do appreciate it."

His grin widened, making those beautiful green eyes glimmer with warmth and humor. "You're welcome, Lokelani."

"I thought you didn't like four-syllable words."

"That one is growing on me." It suddenly felt as though someone had turned the grill up to a high heat, and an awkward moment passed before Puna put an end to it, bless her soul.

"Have you eaten dinner yet, Easton?"

It appeared to take Easton some effort to tear his gaze away from Lani. "No. I was just about to head into town. Which brings us back to the other reason I dropped by. Are there any good places to eat around here?"

"Yes," said Puna before Lani could tell him about her favorite little café. "It's called the Halemahina Pumehana."

Warning bells sounded in Lani's mind, thudding and pounding and crying, *What are you doing, Puna?*

Easton didn't seem to feel the same way because he smiled. "I've heard amazing things about that place. But I thought they only served breakfast there?"

"For you, today we serve dinner too." Puna shooed him inside. "Come on in. We have some fresh tuna steaks in the freezer that can be thawed and grilled in no time."

"When you put it that way, how could I say no?"

Lani stood rooted next to the grill, knowing her reaction bordered on ridiculous. The least they could do was make Easton dinner, and yet Lani couldn't shake the feeling that she'd been blindfolded, spun in circles, and let loose.

By the time she dragged her feet inside, Puna had already put three individually-packaged steaks in a bowl of water to defrost, and she had just picked up her knife to give Easton a lesson on the best way to slice a mango. Based on the way he flicked amused glances her way, Lani was sure he already knew, but he humored Puna regardless, saying things like, "Huh" and "Wow, that really does make it easier. Mahalo, Cora."

Meanwhile, Lani busied herself with adding another plate to the table on the lanai, washing the few dishes remaining in the sink, and getting everything ready for breakfast the following morning.

When the steaks had defrosted, Lani removed them from the plastic bags.

"How are you planning to season them?" Easton asked from behind, causing her body to jolt a little. What was her problem? Even when she'd first begun dating Derek, she'd never been this jittery. Then again, Derek wasn't the sort to creep up behind her or sidle up next to her or tease or flirt or examine her the way Easton did.

She cleared her throat, forcing her mind back to his question. "Salt. Pepper. Lemon. A little garlic."

He peered over her shoulder and assessed the fish. "Those are always good seasonings on fish."

Lani's hand stilled on the container of olive oil as she glanced at him. "There's a 'but' coming, isn't there?"

He shrugged and moved around to face her, leaning his hip against the counter. A smile teased the corners of his

41

mouth. "If you're planning to burn them again, it really doesn't matter what you season them with."

"Keep going on like that and I won't be responsible for the doneness of your fish—or *over*-doneness, I should say."

He chuckled, then chewed on his lower lip for a moment before saying, "How would you feel about learning a new way to cook that? I visited the Azores recently and learned a few things while I was there."

"You visited where?"

"A beautiful island in the middle of the Atlantic. Owned by Portugal. And while I was there, a friend taught me a new way of cooking tuna that I really liked. Figured I could share."

He'd recently visited *another* island? Who was this guy?

She glanced back at the fish and the bottle of olive oil she still held. Truthfully, she was tired of the same tried-and-true lemon, salt, and pepper combo on her fish. Maybe his way of cooking it would taste better. If not, then at least she'd have something to tease him about if he ever brought up burned food again.

Lani stepped to the side and gestured at the steaks. "Teach away."

He hesitated, watching her closely. "I don't want to step on any toes here. You sure you don't mind?"

She almost smiled at that. "It would take a lot more than offering to cook dinner for me to step on my toes."

"Awesome." He clapped his hands then rubbed them together before glancing around the room. From a nearby hook, he grabbed a pink floral apron and put it on, tying the strings behind his back. When he glanced up and caught Lani trying not to laugh, he shrugged and said, "When in Rome . . ."

"Make a dish from another country?" she quipped.

He chuckled and dipped is head in acknowledgement. "Touché."

Lani returned his smile, realizing that for the first time since Easton had walked into the lobby that morning, she felt almost comfortable around him. Almost. Her body was still all-too-much aware of his.

"I have to admit," she said, "pink doesn't look awful on you."

"That's because no color looks awful on me. I get it from my mother." He didn't sound cocky or full of himself, merely confident.

Lani conceded that he was probably right. He was the type of person who could pull off just about anything— maybe even a lava-lava and a floral headdress, though that might be pushing it.

"Have any butter and cayenne pepper?" he asked.

Lani retrieved the ingredients, setting them down on the counter in front of him. "Want me to turn on the grill again?" She could probably use some fresh air—and some distance.

"No grill. We're going to sear these beauties with a frying pan."

Of course they were. She looked wistfully at the door before resigning herself to the too-cozy kitchen. She reached above the stove and grabbed one of the frying pans hanging from a rack, setting it on the counter next to him. "Need anything else?"

"Nope. Just listen, watch, and learn." He picked up the cayenne. "First things first. We're going to season the fish with a few pinches of this and some salt." He glanced over his shoulder. "How spicy do you like your food, Cora?"

"Not too hot and not too bland," came Puna's response.

Easton smiled. "What about you, Lani?"

"I can handle a little more heat."

"Awesome." He coated the steaks with the seasonings, backing off on the cayenne pepper when it came to Puna's. Then he turned up the gas to high and added a little butter and olive oil to the frying pan. As it began to sizzle, he sprinkled in some peppercorns.

Lani watched with interest as he stirred them around in the butter/oil mixture until they softened and popped. Then he tossed in the tuna. "How rare do you ladies like your fish?"

Lani didn't have to look at her grandmother to answer for both of them. "Well done."

Easton glanced at her. "No pink at all?"

"Zero pink."

He shook his head sadly as though he found her answer tragic. "Just when I started to think you both had adventurous sides to you."

"We're about to try fish cooked by a relative stranger who was taught to make it in a country I've never heard of," Lani pointed out. "I'd call that pretty adventurous."

He chuckled. "Touché again. Okay, no pink it is. But you have to at least try a bite of mine." Easton flipped his steak over first, revealing a dark pink, uncooked hue. Lani cringed at the sight, thinking there was no way he'd get her to try that.

Her gaze traveled from the fish up his toned arm and finally landed on his handsome profile. She rested her hip against the counter and said, "What were you doing in the . . . Azarz, was it?"

"Azor-es," he corrected. "And I was visiting."

"Friends?"

"*Making* friends."

"Ever plan to go back?"

"Nope."

"Why not? Didn't you like it?"

"Loved it."

"Then why not go back?"

He shrugged. "I don't know. Been there, done that, I guess. There are a lot of other places to see in this world."

"Like Maui?"

"Exactly." He removed his fish from the pan and slid it onto a plate, then flipped the other two steaks over, revealing golden brown undersides.

Lani covered his plate with tinfoil to keep it warm. "Ever been to Maui before?"

"Once, a long time ago. A friend invited me to come with his family when I was a kid. He was an only child and his parents didn't want him to be bored. We spent the whole time at a resort in Kaanapali, and by the end of the week, we were both sick of the sand."

"Is that why you're back? Because you want to see the rest of the island?"

Easton flipped one of the steaks over, but it wasn't done so he flipped it back. "You ask a lot of questions."

"And you avoid answering most of them."

"What about you?" he said. "What brought you to Hāna?"

So it was back to this. The hard shell that supposedly protected a soft heart. Lani studied him a moment longer before she pushed away from the counter and grabbed the bowl of fruit her grandmother had just finished filling.

"Puna brought me here," she said, purposefully keeping her answer short. Then she smiled warmly at her grandmother before stepping out on the patio where the air was much easier to breathe.

chapter 5

"Easton, this fish is delicious," said Cora. "Mahalo for teaching Lani how to make it."

"Glad you like it." Easton glanced at Lani. Ever since he'd parried all her questions, she'd said very little. Cora had been the one to carry the conversation, telling him about all the sites he should see while in Hāna—sites he'd already read about and seen in countless guidebooks, making them of little interest to him.

Lani, on the other hand, was fascinating. And Cora intrigued him as well.

"I've noticed a lot of paintings on the walls with the same signature," Easton commented as he dug into his incredibly tasty tuna. "I couldn't decipher the name though. Is he or she a famous painter around here?"

"Only famous to my family and some close friends," Cora answered. "They were painted by my late-husband, Kadir."

Ah, so that explained it. Unlike her granddaughter, there was no hint of Polynesian blood in Cora's skin color. Once upon a time, she'd apparently married a native. "I'm sorry to hear he's passed away."

She waved aside his concerns. "It happened a long time ago."

"The paintings are very good. He was a talented man."

She nodded. "The bungalow was actually his studio. He used it to paint all the time. Said it was the most inspiring location in all of Maui."

Lani paused with her fork halfway to her mouth, gaping at her grandmother.

"I can see why he loved it so much," said Easton. "The views from the main room are breathtaking."

"They are breathtaking, but so are the views from here, along with so many other places in Hāna. For Kadir, it wasn't as much about the scenery as the spirit of the place. He always said there was a special feeling in his studio, and every time I visited him while he worked, I felt it too. A mixture of peace and inspiration and . . . a deeper kind of joy, I guess you could say."

Lani set her fork down and clasped her fingers on her lap, watching her grandmother. "Is that why you kept it locked up for so long?"

Cora chuckled and waved a hand in front of her face. "I don't know. After he passed away, I tried going there to feel close to him again, but it only made me feel the loss more. So I locked it up and stayed away."

Lani's expression became one of sympathy and confusion. She obviously hadn't known any of this before and probably didn't appreciate the fact that the answers had come from a conversation Easton had started. He could almost hear the question burning in her eyes. Or maybe he thought that because it was the same question thudding in his mind.

Why had she suddenly decided to reopen the studio for him?

Easton felt like he'd inadvertently opened a Pandora's Box containing stuff that he didn't really want to know.

He shoved the last bite of fish in his mouth and tossed his napkin on his plate. "I think I've taken up enough of your time. I'll rinse my plate and be off. Mahalo for the wonderful dinner."

"But I have guava cake in the fridge I was planning to pull out for dessert," Cora said.

Easton pushed his chair back and stood, patting his stomach to imply he was stuffed. "Sounds delicious, but I couldn't eat another bite. Besides, I have a few things I need to take care of. Rain check?"

"What about tomorrow night? Oh wait. Tomorrow you're going to Ahe's annual summer potluck, aren't you, Lani? Well, maybe Wednesday night then."

Easton heard one thing and one thing only. Annual summer potluck. It captured his attention the way Lani had when he'd first set eyes on her. "Did you just say potluck?"

"Yes," said Lani. "It's a traditional, *local* thing."

In other words, Easton wasn't invited, which didn't surprise him in the least. The aloha spirit only went so far.

"You should take Easton with you," Cora said, coming to his aid. "If he's going to be here the entire summer, it would be a great way for him to meet some of your friends. Otherwise it'll be a lonely three months for him."

"Oh, I'm sure he has more important things to do tomorrow night," said Lani, her tone hinting for him to agree.

Easton ignored it. "Actually, tomorrow night's free and clear. I'd love to be your plus one, Lani."

48

Her jaw clenched the way he figured it might, and her fingers probably itched to strangle him. "I wasn't asked to bring a plus one. And if I had been, Derek would be it."

"But Derek isn't here, dear," Cora said. "You should take Easton and show him what a good time the locals always have."

Lani didn't look too happy about the suggestion.

"Or, if you'd rather not, I suppose Easton can stay here with me and Pearl and perhaps the Cliftons—though I'm sure they'll be off doing something else. Actually, now that I think about it, Pearl was telling me about a game she wanted to teach me called Mahjong. Perhaps you'd like to learn it too, Easton?"

He was quick to shake his head. "A few years ago, I spent some time in the Sichuan Province where I played it often. And truth be told, it's not really my thing. Potlucks, on the other hand . . ." He let the sentence hang there, wishing, hoping, possibly even praying that . . .

Lani finally sighed. "Okay, but you'd better be on your best behavior. Otherwise don't blame me if they literally pick you up and toss you out."

"I'm always on my best behavior," he said.

"That's not very comforting," she said, making him laugh. He'd lost count how many times he'd laughed or smiled or fought back a grin today. Even during the drive to Haiku, his thoughts returned to her and the way she'd looked standing beneath the window with her hair draped across her forehead and falling in soft waves around her shoulders. Her expressive eyes, her smile, her laugh, her spirit, and her determination to keep him at a distance.

Easton found himself smiling yet again. He pushed in his chair and picked up his plate. "Guess I'll see you tomorrow night, Lani."

Her answering nod was slow, cautious. "You can meet me here around six o'clock."

"Perfect." Only one day here, and already he had an "in" with the locals. Not too shabby. "Cora, if you end up enjoying Mahjong, let me know. Even though I don't love the game, I'd be willing to play with you sometime."

Cora reached out to grab a hold of his hand. "I knew when I first heard your voice on the phone that you would be a good fit for the bungalow."

Easton felt a little hitch in his heart, and a small lump lodged in his throat. He'd only known the sweet woman for a matter of hours, but it was obvious she was something special. He gave her hand a squeeze and said, "Mahalo, Cora. Mahalo."

"Easton," came Lani's voice, more tentative this time. "Can I ask you a question before you go?"

"Sure. What's up?"

"What, exactly, do you do for a living?"

The directness of the question caught him off guard. But what did he expect, after casually letting slip that he'd spent time in both the Azores and China? That would make anyone's curiosity meter rise.

Shifting his plate to the other hand, Easton gave it some thought before answering. "I guess you can say I'm sort of an artist, like Kadir. Only instead of picking up a paintbrush to do my work, I pick up my laptop. Goodnight, ladies."

A squeak of the floorboards pulled Lani from her dream of a man with eyes the same color as the deep green of the ocean. She sat up in bed and shoved Easton's face from her mind, refocusing on the noise that had awakened her. She listened and . . . nothing. Had she imagined it, or—

The squeak came again, followed by a heavy sigh.

Lani squinted at the clock and frowned—2:30AM. Why was Puna awake at this hour?

She slipped from her bed and wandered into the hall. A light was on in the main room, so Lani walked toward it, finding her grandmother curled up in her favorite rocker and turning the pages of what appeared to be a small memory book of pictures.

The floor squeaked as Lani crossed it. "Everything okay?"

Her grandmother continued looking at one picture in particular. Her aged fingers touched the plastic covering lightly. "I just couldn't sleep is all. I'm sorry if I woke you."

Lani pulled up a chair and took a seat at her grandmother's side. "What are you looking at?"

"Some very old pictures of me and Kadir. It's been too long since I've opened this album." She pointed at a picture of a younger version of her standing next to a large and handsome Hawaiian man. She was holding a fishing pole with a large fish dangling from the end of the line. "He took me fishing for my first time, and that's what I reeled in. Isn't that amazing? I determined then and there that I would live in Hawaii the rest of my life."

Lani had never seen the picture before—or the one on the page next to it, with both of her grandparents standing next to a burning torch, wearing beautiful leis. "Where was that?"

"Kadir's best friend's wedding. We were engaged at the time and planning our own. The four of us used to do so much together." Puna flipped the page, and there she was, dressed in a long and simple, beautiful white dress with a lei around her shoulders. Her once-dark hair had been pulled back into a bun, with a plumeria tucked beside it.

Lani fingered the edge of the page. "You made a beautiful bride, Puna."

Her grandmother pointed to the next picture. "And Kadir made a beautiful groom, didn't he? Oh, how he made my heart soar."

Lani felt a constriction in her chest. How many times would she have loved to sit at her grandmother's side and flip through old photo books, listening to all the memories of her late-grandfather—a man who'd died nearly fifteen years ago? Until today, every time Lani had brought him up, her questions had been redirected and the subject changed.

And then an almost-stranger came to dinner, asked one question, and suddenly Kadir became as casual a topic of conversation as a discussion about the weather. Lani had never felt more confused, or, she had to admit, hurt. Ever since dinner, something had gnawed and pestered, refusing to ease up.

"Puna, why did you tell Easton about Grandfather's studio and the paintings?"

"I was telling you both."

Lani shook her head. "No, otherwise you would have mentioned it before tonight. I have asked so many questions about *Kapuna,* and you've deflected them all until now. Why?"

Her grandmother closed the book gently, keeping it clutched in her hands on her lap. She stared at the wall across from her, and her body slowly rocked back and forth. "It's hard to talk about him without feeling lost. And I don't like to feel lost or sad—not when there's so much to be happy about."

Lani could understand that. In the five years she'd lived with her grandmother, she couldn't remember ever seeing

Puna sad or even imagine it. Her grandmother thrived on giving, loving, sharing, and doing. "Then why was it okay to tell Easton? Why is it okay to talk to me about him now?"

A soft smile touched Cora's face, and she laid her head against the back of the rocker. "I should probably tell you the real reason I decided to rent Kadir's studio."

Lani said nothing, only waited for her grandmother to continue.

"It began like I told you. Pearl mentioned what a shame it was that we didn't rent out the little house on the hill, and the phone rang. When I first heard Easton's voice, my heart nearly stopped. He sounded exactly like Kadir. And that's when I knew it was time. It were as if Kadir was telling me himself that I'd kept his memory buried long enough."

Lani didn't know what to make of it all, but it made her happy that Puna had found a reason to unbottle the painful memories that had been trapped inside her for so long. "And you couldn't have told me that while we were cleaning?"

Puna patted her hand. "Baby steps, my dear. At the time, it was all I could do to turn the key in the lock."

"And tonight at dinner? Did Easton still sound like Grandfather?"

A throaty chuckle sounded, and Puna shook her head. "Not at all. Isn't that interesting? Mostly it was his personality that reminded me of Kadir."

"Really?"

Her grandmother nodded, pushing with her feet so that her rocker swayed back and forth. "Kadir used to enjoy teasing me the way Easton teased you tonight. He wasn't afraid to make a stand or push me beyond what others considered my limits. And my, was he charming. The man could make my heart drop to my toes with a simple look or touch or smile—just like Easton did to you."

Whoa. Puna had jerked a lovely conversation onto rocky terrain, and Lani was not okay with it. Her name belonged next to Derek's—not Easton's or anyone else's. "Puna, don't be silly. My heart never dropped to my toes."

Her grandmother directed a pointed look at Lani. "You burned the fish. You *never* burn fish."

"That had nothing to do with Easton. I was in the kitchen talking to you—not him."

"You can't deny that you've been in a state of distraction ever since that man walked through the door."

"Only because nothing has made sense since, until now—the bungalow, Pearl, Easton. Actually, it still isn't clear. So if I burn any more fish, *that's* why. Not because a well-traveled, invitation-finagling mystery man shows up on the doorstep. I don't get swept off my feet that easily—just look at me and Derek."

Puna laughed the way Lani hadn't heard her laugh in a long while, like it had been cowering deep, too afraid to come out until now. "I have been looking, and you're right. Derek hasn't done any sweeping that I can tell."

Lani sighed and gave her grandmother's shoulder a squeeze before standing. It was late, she was tired, and breakfast still needed to be made in the morning. "Goodnight, *kapuna wahine*," she said, using the formal name for grandmother.

Puna stopped rocking and grabbed hold of Lani's hand, keeping her from leaving. "There's a reason Easton has come for the summer. I think he's here to teach your heart how to soar. Please let him, Lani. There's nothing so magical as soaring."

Lani felt shaky and weary all of a sudden, as though her legs couldn't keep her upright much longer. "Puna, I'm engaged to Derek, and I'm going to marry him. The only soaring I will be doing is flying over the Pacific on my way back to him in three months. I need you to come to terms with that and not spend the entire summer trying to throw me at someone who will be in and out of both of our lives. No good will come of it, I promise you that."

Puna smiled in a tolerant way and gave Lani's hand one last pat. "*Aloha auinapo, kealoha.*"

Lani gently pulled her hand free and walked back to bed. It was a long time before she fell asleep, and when she did, her dreams were filled with hearts sprouting wings and flapping high into the sky, soaring over the ocean and right past California.

She woke up feeling like she hadn't slept at all.

chapter 6

L ani tried not to fret about her reflection in the mirror. She also tried to convince herself that the reason she'd taken extra care with her appearance had nothing to do with Easton Allard. She was wearing her favorite pink, floral sarong because Ahe had given it to her. And the reason it had taken four attempts to finally get the loose French braid to flow around her head in an attractive slant was because she didn't want it falling out halfway through the night.

It was.

She gave herself a firm look in the mirror and adjusted her white cotton top yet again. *You love Derek Lundstrom. You love Derek Lundstrom. You're going to move back to California for Derek Lundstrom.*

Two lines appeared between her brows, proof that she was fretting yet again. Only this time, it had nothing to do with her appearance and everything to do with her heart's recent state of confusion.

She rubbed the area of her left ring finger where an

engagement ring would soon rest as a symbol of her commitment to a man who'd been nothing but loyal to her. She did love Derek. No, it wasn't the soaring kind of love her grandmother spoke of, and maybe it never would be. But it was a solid love built on years of friendship and trust. It was the kind of love that would last. She needed to remember that and remind her heart of it whenever it decided to beat too fast for someone else.

Lani studied her reflection before she slowly tugged the elastic from the end of her hair. Then she combed her fingers through the perfected braid, leaving her hair wavy and untamed around her face. She wiped off some eye-liner, slipped out of the pretty wedge sandals, and pushed her feet into a pair of faded pink flip-flops. She kept the sarong out of respect to Ahe. She knew how much time and money he and his family invested in this party every year.

On her way out, Lani stopped in the kitchen to grab the fruit salad she'd made earlier, a recipe from the mainland that her local friends loved, then walked out to the lanai, determined to not let her eyes or her heart wander any further than they already had. But the moment she saw Easton, it was like a hundred butterflies broke free from their cocoons in her chest, flapping and fluttering and beating their wings.

He sat casually in the chair, wearing a baseball hat, green t-shirt, and board shorts. He definitely hadn't redone his hair four times, tried on three outfits, or took ten minutes to decide on the simple black flip-flops he wore. And yet he looked good. Really good. Too good.

Easton stood and grabbed a plastic sack filled with something yellow and red and smiled at her. "You look gorgeous tonight, Lokelani. I hope you didn't dress up just for me."

"I dressed up for Ahe," she said, hoping it really was the truth.

He lifted an eyebrow. "Who's Ahe? Does Derek know about him?"

"Yes, Derek knows about him. Ahe is my very good friend. He welcomed me to Hāna when I showed up five years ago and is a great fisherman. He brings us freshly caught fish about once a week." She bypassed Easton and stepped down to the gravel, lava rock-lined path. "We should go. The party started hours ago."

"What? Wait up." Easton jogged to catch up and fell into step beside her. "Why are we going now if it started hours ago?"

"It's been going on all day, but I have something called a job that I couldn't leave until now." She cursed her wayward heart for skipping a beat every time his shoulder brushed against hers. The gravel path was wide. Why did he have to walk so close? Why did he have to smell like ivory soap mixed with a tantalizing, sporty-scented aftershave?

She turned her head into the breeze and took a long whiff of the white hibiscus, trying to clear her senses.

When they arrived at her grandmother's once-red 1988 Chevy LUV, Easton said, "We can take my rental if you want."

"Ahe's family won't recognize your car, so it'll be easier to take this. Parking is going to be a little crazy."

Easton nodded, waited for her to climb inside, then closed her door and jogged around to the other side. She already had her window rolled down by the time he'd hopped in beside her.

She turned the key, and the powerful engine roared to life. "What are your plans for tomorrow?" she asked.

"Not sure yet. Any suggestions?"

"That all depends on what you and your laptop do together."

He chuckled. "I type. It responds. We repeat."

"What do you type?" She raised her voice to be heard above the car. "Numbers? Letters? Characters?"

"Mostly letters and words. Sentences. Paragraphs. That sort of thing."

At least he was *sort of* answering her questions today, Lani thought as she reversed the truck. "So you're a writer."

"Yes."

She shot him a quick sideways look before turning onto the highway. "That wasn't so hard to say, was it?"

"Actually, it was. I had to force the words out in a painful, torturous way. Please don't ask me anything else or my mouth might not be able to handle it."

She ignored him, keeping her eyes on the road. "What sort of writer? Oh wait, let me guess. You're a novelist. You have a deadline to meet by the end of the summer and you've chosen Hāna as the place to inspire that future *New York Times* bestselling tale. Am I right?"

He'd rolled down his window, and his arm hung outside, his hand rising and dipping in the wind. "You'll take away all my fun if you make me admit it out loud."

Lani shot him another look, trying to read his expression. "You're really a novelist?" It made sense. Why would anyone choose to spend their entire summer in such an out-of-the-way place as Hāna unless they wanted a location that was quiet and remote? "Or maybe you're on the run from some sort of law enforcement agency," Lani said. "Hāna is a good place to hide if you don't want to be found."

"Personally, I think you should be the novelist. You've obviously got a great imagination."

"Seriously," she said. "You're really a writer?"

"I really am. And, believe it or not, I do have an important end-of-summer deadline looming." His words sounded genuine, and his tone held a hint of stress, as though the deadline was coming faster than he wanted it to come.

"What sort of stories do you write?" she asked. "Fantasy? Sci-Fi? Suspense? Horror? No wait—you write romance, don't you? That would explain why you're so secretive about it."

He chuckled. "You figured me out. I am a closet romance novelist."

"No really. What do you write?" Lani was genuinely interested. The only other writer she'd ever met was a little woman from Iowa who had come to Hāna to work on a memoir. She'd been much more open than Easton, and her life had been fascinating.

"A little of this, a little of that." His hand was back inside the car, playing with the handles of the plastic sack he carried.

"What would happen if I googled the name 'Easton Allard'?"

"You'd find nada, which I'm sure you already know."

Lani rolled her eyes. "Give me a break. I haven't googled your name, nor will I."

"Ouch. Your honesty, while refreshing, is doing very cruel things to my ego." His twitching lips showed that he hadn't taken it too hard.

She forged on, "Well, if Google doesn't know about you, then you must not have a social media presence, which I can't believe. So that means you probably write under a different name."

"Ding, ding, ding." Easton grinned. "You nailed it again. I'm an infamous, closet-romance-writing, fraud. Whew. I'm glad that's out of the way. Can we still be friends?"

She lifted an eyebrow, trying not to laugh. "Is *he* well known?"

"Who?"

"Your pen name."

"Oh." He shrugged, returning his attention to the view of the coast out his window. "He. She. Does it matter? Will you only be my friend if my alter-ego is famous?"

The wind whipped Lani's hair into her face. She pushed it aside and glanced at Easton's profile, trying to figure out how much of what he'd said was fact or fiction. Was he really a novelist? Somehow, the profession fit, so Lani decided to take his cryptic word for it. Writers travelled. Writers migrated toward remote locations. Writers—or at least bestselling writers—made decent money, didn't they? That's why he could afford to travel so much?

She really had no idea.

Regardless, it made sense like nothing else had since she'd met him.

"What's your pen name?" she asked.

A moment of silence met her question before he answered. "Only a handful of people will ever know that— my mom, dad, siblings, and future bride. Since you've made it clear you're already taken, well . . . sorry."

Lani swiped away the hair that had blown into her mouth and smiled. "I'm glad you finally understand that. I was worried you never would."

She could feel his gaze on her profile, watching, assessing, and thinking. And then he said, "So where is this Derek guy, and why hasn't he hopped on that plane you mentioned and put a ring on your finger? What's he waiting for?"

Lani glanced at the fourth finger on her left hand, the one Derek's ring would soon circle. It suddenly felt as though

61

it was already there, but way too tight and cutting off her circulation. Her fingers tapped the steering wheel one after another, like she was playing a simple tune on the piano, then clenched together and released.

What was wrong with her? Most girls dreamed of the day a handsome man would slip a beautiful diamond ring on their finger. Why couldn't Lani feel the giddiness, the excitement, the joy? Why wasn't she ordering bridal magazines, making wedding plans, and thinking of flowers and bridesmaids and cake?

"Well?" Easton said, reminding her that she'd left him hanging.

She drew in a breath. "He *was* here. Last week. That's when he proposed, and I agreed to move back to California at the end of the summer. We'll make it official once I get there."

"So when you said the ring was coming by plane, what you really meant was *you're* the one who will be traveling by plane."

"Ding, ding, ding," she mimicked.

His attention returned to the passing trees that hid Hāna Bay from sight. "Know what else you said?"

"What?"

"That you're not officially engaged." Even though she couldn't see his face, she heard the all's-fair-until-it's-official smile in his voice, and the sound of it felt more constricting and unsettling than the imagined ring on her finger.

"Who's the haole?" asked a large, Polynesian man from his perch on the log next to a fire pit, directing the question at Lani. With black, curly hair that hung below his ears and shoulders the size of a linebacker's, he didn't have to stand for Easton to know he was tall. The ukulele he held looked more like a child's toy than a legitimate instrument, and the wary expression on his face told Easton that he'd taken an instant dislike to the newcomer. On either side of him sat three other men, one wider, one narrower, and one completely bald.

Behind the group was a swarm of Polynesians, and next to several tables coated in food, two men were digging up what Easton assumed was a *kalua*—an underground oven. He watched with interest while breathing in the tantalizing smell of barbeque.

"Which haole are you talking about, Ahe?" said Lani. "Him or me?"

That brought a smile to Ahe's face. He set down the instrument and stood, clasping Lani's shoulders and giving her a peck on the cheek. "*Aznuts*, Lani. You know you my *sistah*. What took you so long?"

"I had to work, which you already know." She gestured toward Easton. "This is Easton Allard. He'll be staying at the Halemahina Pumehana for the summer, so I invited him to come along. Easton, this is Ahe, our host, along with Rab, Lajos, and Paavo."

"Good to meet you." Easton held out his hand to be polite, but wasn't surprised when Ahe ignored it and offered him a head-nod instead. Easton let his hand fall back to his side, wondering how long it had taken Lani to earn the title of *sistah*. From the way Ahe looked at her with something more than admiration, probably not too long. The woman apparently had more than a few admirers.

"Where do you want this?" Lani held up the bowl she carried.

Ahe waved at the tables already packed with food before returning to take a seat next to his friends. Lani left to find a place for her bowl, leaving Easton alone.

A heavy-set woman in a flowing purple muumuu walked his way, carrying a large bowl of rice. She slowed when she got to Easton. "Aloha. You come with Lani?"

"I did," Easton answered. "Can I help you with that?"

"No, no. I'm okay. What's that you got there?"

Easton followed her gaze to the bag he'd almost forgotten he brought.

He pulled the packages out and smiled. "The cashier at the store mentioned they were a local favorite."

"Ah, Starbursts!" The woman smiled in return, revealing a mouthful of white, crooked teeth. Changing her mind about wanting his help, she handed Easton the bowl of rice and clutched the treat to her ample chest. "My favorite. Mahalo."

"Mahalo for having me." Easton figured there would be more than enough food to go around, so he'd brought a few large bags of candy instead. He followed her to a table and waited while she rearranged a few plates and bowls to make room for the rice. As soon as he set it down, she waved him away. "Now go find Lani, eat much, and have fun."

Easton shoved his hands into his pockets and scanned the throng. Ahe and his friends had left the log and were now carving meat from the roasted pig. Lani stood not far away, chatting with a few women. She gestured for him to join her, which he did, and was soon introduced to more people. Most offered him a friendly "Aloha," then seemed to forget all about him. Easton wasn't surprised. It was a tight-knit community built around years, even generations, of connections. He was an outsider.

Eventually, he and Lani were handed plates and shooed

in the direction of the food. After the two months he'd spent in Arcaju, Brazil, without gaining a taste for taro, he knew to stay away from the *lau lau* and *poi*, and instead loaded up on rice, *kalua* pig, Lani's fruit salad, and *malasada*—the sugar donut equivalent.

When his plate could hold no more, Lani led him to a table filled with women, and they sat on the end. She did most of the talking while Easton was content to listen and eat. Halfway through the meal, the woman next to Lani leaned toward him and said, "Where you come from, Easton?"

He swallowed the food in his mouth before answering. "Boston area."

"Boston? *Fo real?*" Before he could answer, she pointed to another woman and said, "Ho, remember when Taavatti wen go stay Boston and get a *rat bite?*"

Laughter erupted up and down the table, and even Lani giggled. Her shoulder touched his as she leaned in to whisper, "A 'rat bite' is a really awful haircut. And it was awful. Trust me."

It didn't escape Easton's notice that Lani had voluntarily touched him. Usually, she shied away, stepped away, or backed away, but not this time. Easton had been aware of everything about Lani since he'd met her. Even now, he couldn't stop looking at her from the corner of his eyes and appreciating what he saw. The way her dark hair splayed across her collarbone, the way her shoulders trembled when she laughed, and the way her nose turned up a tad at the end. It fit her the way her skirt fit her hips.

More to test the waters than make conversation, Easton let his shoulder touch hers, "How long did it take you to learn Hawaiian Creole?"

She looked at him in surprise, not shying away from his

touch at all. He held back a smile. Was she actually warming up to him?

"Here they call it Pidgin."

"But it's not a pidgin, at least not anymore. It started off that way, but over time it's evolved into more of a creole language."

She shifted positions so her shoulder wasn't touching his anymore. "You've obviously done your research." The way she said it made it sound a bit like censure.

"I always do my research." And he did. His e-reader was filled with dozens of books about Hawaii—everything from travel guides to history books to culture. That's how he'd known he should bring something to contribute to the potluck tonight—preferably something that came from the mainland.

"Then you should also know that the aloha spirit is very real here. These people are wonderful and good and welcoming. They don't need—or deserve—a linguistics lesson."

Despite the rebuff, Easton's opinion of Lani rose. He admired her loyalty and how she wasn't afraid to stand up for her friends. That said, she'd obviously misunderstood his intention.

"For what it's worth, I didn't mean it as an insult," said Easton. "I was just trying to impress you with my knowledge."

She looked as though she might not believe him. "Kindness impresses me more than intelligence."

"Duly noted."

"Not that you should care about impressing me," she amended.

"Oh, but I do, Lokelani," Easton said in all honesty, unable to resist sweeping back a stray lock of hair from in front of her eye. "I haven't figured out exactly why yet, but I do."

A faint blush appeared on her cheeks, and she quickly looked away, inching another few inches to her right.

So much for progress.

Easton forked another pile of *kalua* pig into his mouth, wondering what it was about Lani that intrigued him. He'd known plenty of beautiful, spirited, and intelligent women, but none had drawn his interest or notice more than her.

Why? He couldn't figure it out.

Eventually someone threw several logs in the pit and started a small fire. In the distance, the sky above Haleakalā was a rich and textured array of blues, purples, yellows, reds, and oranges.

"Lani, over here!" Ahe's voice called a few minutes later. He sat with his back facing the sunset, apparently more interested in the beauty in front of him than behind. "You need to sing for us."

"I'm eating," Lani said, picking up the plastic fork that had been resting on her plate for a while.

Easton felt the need to point that out. "If you're worried about leaving those last few crumbs, don't. I'll take care of them for you." If Lani could sing, he wanted to hear it.

"I don't want to sing."

"Oh, sure you do." He took the fork from her and put it back on her plate, which he then stacked on top of his. "I know how much you love to do things for Ahe. Isn't that why you wore that skirt? Or was it really for me? Because if that's the case, I'd rather you stay right here and not sing."

Her glare flashed to him before her chin rose and a look of determination crossed her face. She handed him her used napkin and stood, saying nothing as she walked to Ahe's side and took a seat next to him on the log.

They exchanged a few words, and Ahe grinned, nodding in approval at her choice of song. Then he began strumming his ukulele. As the first few chords lifted into the air, the men began cheering and the women laughed. Apparently everyone recognized the song but Easton.

Lani's eyes connected with his in silent challenge as she began to sing, her voice light and airy.

Green eyes and light hair can't woo me
'Cause I'm too crazy about the local boys
You can try, but my heart is steady
'Cause the local boys are all killahz.

Easton chuckled as she sang, liking her spunk and the way the light from the flames danced in her eyes and highlighted her hair. The song wasn't long—just a few verses—and when it ended the crowd whistled and clapped, then begged for more. Lani tried to stand, but Ahe's hand captured her wrist, keeping her at his side.

She conceded. "One more, and that's it."

This time Ahe chose the song, and it was one Easton recognized. "Island Style" by John Cruz. He sat back and folded his arms, his gaze still on Lani. The sunset was nearly gone, pushed away by the dusk settling in and paving the way for darkness to claim the skies. The airiness in Lani's voice became denser and more beautiful. It swept up and around, quieting voices and commanding attention. Her eyelids fluttered closed and her body swayed as she sang. Others joined in, and a feeling of serenity and camaraderie settled around Easton. It occurred to him that *this* was the true aloha spirit of Hawaii. He'd read about it, thought he knew what it meant, but now he *felt* it. The love, the acceptance, the soul-touching joy. It embraced him and everyone else, bonding them together.

Wanting to capture the moment, Easton pulled his phone from his pocket and snapped a picture of Lani.

When the song ended, the large woman wearing the purple muumuu grasped his shoulders and leaned over him.

"How you get Lani to sing? She *never* sings for a crowd."

"It was Ahe who got her to sing. Not me."

"No. Ahe always teases, and she always says no. But today, you wen say somet'ing, and she sings so pretty. For dat, you always welcome at my table." She gave his shoulder a solid pat and bustled away.

Eyes drawn to Lani yet again, Easton caught her looking at him. For a moment, their gazes locked, and he felt an almost palpable connection between them—one that snapped and popped and sizzled. And then Ahe said something to her and it severed. She shook her head in the negative, then stood, moving away from Ahe, in the opposite direction from Easton.

An impulse urged him to follow, but Easton resisted, letting her go.

chapter 7

E aston tossed the empty plates in a metal garbage bin and looked around. The woman with the purple muumuu had opened the packages of the Starbursts he'd brought and dumped the individual pieces in a turquoise bowl. A few people walking by took a small handful, and Easton followed suit. Then he wandered over to the perimeter of the yard, squinted through the darkness, and finally spotted a few twigs on the ground beneath some shrubs. He snatched one up and broke the tip off.

Easton returned to the fire, where Ahe was strumming the ukulele again and several people were singing along. A group of young adults had gathered around, and sparks flew as one of Ahe's friends threw another log on. The seats were all taken, so Easton walked over to the group, found an opening between two logs and two girls, and crouched down. He unwrapped a cherry-flavored starburst, speared it with the stick, and held it over the fire. The girls on each side of him watched with curiosity.

"*'Ey, lolo,*" called one of Ahe's friends, nodding toward Easton. "Wot you doin'?"

"Fishing," Easton answered dryly.

The guy laughed until Ahe's elbow shut him up. "Seriously, haole, wot dat Starburst do to you?"

Easton's legs were beginning to cramp, so he sat back and lifted the stick from the fire. He blew on the candy for a moment before biting it off the end of the stick. The now-gooey fruity flavor coated his tongue before he swallowed it.

"Haven't you ever roasted a Starburst?" he asked.

Ahe's friend looked interested.

"Can I try?" One of the girls next to him pointed at the stick. Easton handed it to her, then held out a handful of candy, allowing her to pick her favorite flavor. She chose lemon. Easton unwrapped it for her, pushed it on the end of the stick, and everyone watched as it changed from matte to glossy.

After a few minutes, Easton said, "Looks good enough to eat."

She blew on it a few times before popping it into her mouth. Then she smiled and nodded. "*Ho, dat's trippy, l'dat.*"

The positive review sent several of the others searching for their own twigs, and before long, a colorful array of Starbursts hung over the fire. Only Ahe and his friends weren't participating.

"What's going on?" Lani's voice sounded behind him.

"Ho, Lani, your *lolo* haole make us crazy like him," said one of the guys as he blew on an orange Starburst.

Easton craned his neck up until he saw her, then grinned. "Care for a roasted Starburst?"

Her lips twitched slightly. "Um . . . no. I'm good, thanks."

He shrugged and returned his attention to the orange-flavored candy that he held over the fire.

Lani crouched next to him and dropped her voice. "You ready to go anytime soon? My day starts early tomorrow."

Easton immediately handed his stick to the girl on his left. "Looks like I gotta go."

"Mahalo," she said, accepting the stick.

Easton pried himself off the ground and swiped the dust from his shorts. Then he nodded at the group. "Mahalo, Ahe. It's been fun."

Ahe responded with a quick nod at Easton and an "Aloha" for Lani, then returned his attention to the ukulele.

Others waved as they left, and the large woman in purple, who had never introduced herself, was the last to say, "Aloha, Lani and Easton. Come again."

Easton was touched that she'd made the effort to learn his name. After Lani hugged the woman goodbye, he hugged her as well, saying, "Mahalo." As soon as they were alone in Lani's truck, Easton found out the woman was Ahe's mother, and her name was Kaia.

Lani didn't speak much on the drive home, and Easton didn't either. Instead, he unrolled the window and let the fresh air fill the silence. When they pulled in the drive, Lani tugged the key from the ignition and hopped out.

Easton met her in front of the truck. "Thanks for taking me with you tonight. I know you didn't want to, but it was a night I'll never forget, and . . . well, I appreciate it."

"No problem."

She started past him, and without really meaning to, Easton reached out and touched her arm. She stopped and stiffened, glancing back at him. "Yes?"

He had no idea what to say or why he'd felt the need to detain her. The easy camaraderie they'd shared on the way into town had hardened into a formality he didn't like. He wanted to go forward with Lani, not backward.

Unfortunately, she didn't feel the same. So he let his hand drop to his side, and he took a step back. "*Moe malie*, Lani."

Her eyes widened slightly before she recovered. "I hope you sleep well too. Good night."

Her flip-flops scuffed against the gravel, and her shadow danced behind her. She paused at the door and looked back only briefly before walking inside.

Easton could smell the gentle perfume of the flowers along the walk, and somewhere, leaves rustled. The hammock was calling his name. So he shoved his hands into his pockets and was about to head to his bungalow when he heard footsteps.

He turned around to find a petite, older Asian woman behind him. There was something familiar about her that he couldn't place, and yet he didn't think he'd ever seen her before. She had a sense of timelessness about her, as though he could pick her up, drop her in any era, and she'd fit right in.

"Lovely night, isn't it?" She had a mild Chinese accent.

"Yes," he said. "Are you a guest here as well?"

She nodded. "I'm Pearl. And you are?"

"Easton Allard." She must be the woman Cora mentioned was teaching her Mahjong. He held out his hand for her to shake, which she did. Then she nodded in the direction Lani had gone, and something in her hair caught the light and glinted. It looked like a grouping of pearls embedded in a comb.

"Was that Lani you were talking to?"

"Yeah. We just got back from a local potluck thing."

"I hope you enjoyed yourself."

Easton's gaze gravitated toward the house where Lani had disappeared inside. "I did. It was . . . enlightening."

"I find it interesting that sometimes it takes the sun going down to see more clearly."

Her words made Easton think of dusk framing Lani as she sang and the warm glow that had enveloped him. "I think you might be right."

She clasped her fingers together in front of her. "What are your plans for the rest of the week?"

"I'm not sure. Any suggestions?"

Pearl shrugged. "How do you feel about fishing?"

"Fishing?" Easton had been fishing one too many times in his life. He could think of ten thousand things he'd rather do than stand on a dock with a pole and wait. He'd never understood what drew so many people to that sport, if you could call it a sport.

"I hear there's good fishing to be found in Hāna Bay, and I noticed a small dingy through the window of the shed over there. Maybe you could give it a try. Though I wouldn't go tomorrow. The forecast is predicting high winds."

Easton rubbed the back of his neck. "I have to be honest, I'm not much of a—"

"I hear Lani is quite good at fishing. Maybe she could go along and give you a few pointers?"

Suddenly, fishing didn't sound so boring. It sounded enticing and riveting and even fun. Easton smiled. "You might be on to something, Pearl, though I have the feeling that Lani probably won't be interested, not if I'm in the boat with her."

Pearl's expression became thoughtful, and a few seconds passed before she said, "I think Lani is very protective of her heart. She won't give it away to just anyone."

"Ah, but she already has—to a guy named Derek who lives in California."

Pearl tilted her head to the side and peered at him, looking beyond his eyes and into what felt like his soul. What she found seemed to satisfy her, and she squinted toward her cottage. "Perhaps part of her heart, but I don't think all of it. She keeps the most precious and tender part locked tight. It'll take the right man—a special man—to find a way inside."

Easton chuckled because he didn't know what else to say. Was she implying that he was that man, or should try to be that man? No. Easton wasn't interested in finding his way into Lani's heart. He simply wanted to borrow a portion of it for a while then give it back at the end of the summer, at which time Derek would be more than welcome to it. Easton wasn't in this for keeps. He wasn't in anything for keeps. That's how things worked in his life; how they had to work.

But deep down, he already knew that come the end of the summer, it might not be so easy to walk away this time.

"I can see you have much to think about, so I will leave you to it." Pearl smiled and dipped her head, then strode past him, walking gracefully back to her cottage.

Easton was left mulling over the aftertaste of a very strange and interesting conversation. Forcing his feet up the grassy slope to his bungalow, he drew in a deep breath and pulled out his phone, going straight to the picture he'd taken of Lani singing. It was dark and slightly out of focus, but as he looked at her face and the people clustered around her, he was reminded of the feeling she'd brought to the group—to him.

Something in his mind shifted, and for the first time since his plane landed in Maui, Easton was glad he'd wound up here. This was the reason he traveled, the reason he sought out and befriended the locals in every country he'd ever been to. Despite language barriers and cultural differences, each experience changed him for the better. And tonight, he had definitely been changed.

The hammock no longer called out to him, so he bypassed it and went inside the bungalow instead. As he crawled onto the stiff and uncomfortable bed and rested his head on the pathetic excuse for a pillow, rather than thinking about melted, fruit-flavored candy or Hawaiian music or food, food, and more food, his thoughts veered to Lani.

When he finally fell asleep, he dreamed of keys and a lock in the shape of a heart.

chapter 8

L ani scooped the last omelet on a plate, picked up a set of napkin-wrapped utensils, and carried it out to the lanai. All the guests had shown up within fifteen minutes of each other, including the Murphys, who had checked in late last night. Due to yet another cancellation, Pearl was still with them.

When Lani had told her the good news, Pearl had smiled in her calm, serene way, and clasped her fingers in front of her waist—her only show of surprise. "Oh, what Providence."

"Yes. Providence," Lani had said, not sure what to make of the woman. She couldn't help but think of her grandmother's comment about how most events in life weren't happenstance, and for a moment, Lani had felt a seed of belief weave its way into her soul. But then she shook it off as ludicrous. Of course Pearl's continued stay was a coincidence. She couldn't control another guest's decision to cancel a reservation.

But it was odd that guests continued to cancel and she continued to stay.

From the corner of her eye, Lani watched Pearl chat with her grandmother. The two spent a lot of time these days with heads bent together, and every time Lani asked her grandmother what they talked about, she would say, "Life, dear. Just life. Pearl is a very interesting woman."

Lani couldn't argue with that.

Suddenly, her hip whacked into something hard, and Lani stumbled to the side to keep her balance. When her elbow connected with Easton's head, the slippery omelet slid from the plate, careened down Easton's forehead and face, finally landing on his lap.

Lani's mouth dropped open, and she covered it with her free hand. "Oh, I'm so sorry!"

Easton glanced from the omelet massacre to her and pasted on a smile. "No worries. I'd rather wear an omelet than eat one, anyway."

His meaning took a second to register. "You don't like omelets?"

"Not really, no."

"Why didn't you say so?"

"Because I didn't want to be rude. But now that you've tossed one on me, I'm feeling like I can be honest. So no, I don't like omelets. I don't really like to wear them either."

Lani glanced around at the other guests. Mr. and Mrs. Murphy were hunched forward, shoulders shaking, obviously trying not to laugh out loud, and Pearl and Puna watched with wide-open amusement.

Lani was mortified.

Easton tugged the plate from her hand and scooped what he could of the omelet off his lap, throwing it back on the plate. Not knowing what else to do, Lani quickly unwound the napkin from the utensils and held it out, feeling helpless. She wasn't about to help wipe up the remaining egg bits from his lap.

Desperate to do something to make it up to him, she asked, "What do you like for breakfast?"

"My favorite is a large bowl full of Lucky Charms."

"Seriously?" She never knew for sure with him.

"Deadly."

"Really?"

"I don't know how you can get more deadly than deadly."

"But . . ." Did they even sell Lucky Charms at the general store? Lani had no idea. She only knew that they didn't have any in their cupboards at the moment. "Anything else?" she asked, trying to think of what they did have. "Yogurt? Fruit? Oatmeal? Banana bread?"

He grinned. "I happen to love oatmeal and banana bread."

"You're not just saying that because you don't want to be rude?"

He shook his head. "I think the omelet has taken our relationship to a new level of openness. I really do like oatmeal. With lots of brown sugar and a sprinkle of cinnamon. I'm even pretty good at making it myself if you show me where—"

"No, no. I can handle it." Lani grabbed the plate and headed back inside, pausing in the doorway to glance back. "Anyone else not like omelets and would prefer some oatmeal?"

"These omelets are divine," said Mrs. Murphy. "Pat and I were just talking about how delicious they are. I think if this young man had been able to taste a bite, he might have changed his mind about not liking them."

Lani gave Mrs. Murphy a grateful smile. "Thank you," she said. "But as I said to everyone at check-in, if there's anything on the morning menu that you don't like, please"— she shot Easton a pointed glance—"let me know."

He offered her a salute before she went inside.

By the time Lani had cooked a bowl of oatmeal and returned to the lanai, the Murphys had left and Easton had washed his hair and changed clothes. She set the bowl in front of him, along with a small plate of fruit and some extra brown sugar just in case she hadn't sweetened it enough.

"Mahalo," he said. "This looks great."

"You're welcome. Will there be anything else?"

"Actually, yeah." His gaze darted over to where Pearl and Puna still sat chatting, and he cleared his throat, raising his voice a notch. "I noticed a small boat in the shed off the driveway and wondered if you loan it out."

"You want to go boating?"

Pearl and Puna had stopped talking, no doubt suddenly interested in Lani and Easton's exchange. Easton cleared his throat again. "Fishing, actually. I'm hoping you might have a rod for me to borrow as well."

"You like to fish?"

His eyes flickered to the other women again before returning to her. "Love it," he said.

For whatever reason, the news surprised Lani. Which was silly. Of course he enjoyed fishing. He was a writer and probably enjoyed any pastime that gave him opportunities to think.

"Kadir loved to fish too," said Puna, making it obvious they were eavesdropping. "You'll find some old rods of his hanging next to the boat in the shed. His tackle box is on the shelf above. Feel free to use whatever you'd like. Lani has the key."

"Sounds great." He squinted up at Lani. "Care to join me?"

"Um . . ." She hadn't been expecting an invite, so it took her a moment to think of an excuse—the vague kind that sounded as made up as it was. "Sorry, but my afternoon is pretty booked."

It wasn't a complete lie. The lobby was past due for a good dusting, and she'd noticed some weeds growing near the front door.

"Lani, that's nonsense," said Puna in her unhelpful way. "Nothing needs doing that can't wait until tomorrow. Go and have fun. Live a little. Easton will need our truck to transport the boat to the bay anyway."

Easton grinned, apparently happy with Puna's comment. Well of course he was. It meant that he won and Lani lost. Who wouldn't be happy about that?

Lani glared at her grandmother. "I thought you wanted to prune the bushes on the side of the house before it got too hot."

Puna waved her off. "That can wait. I'm enjoying myself here. Which is exactly my point. You should enjoy yourself too."

"It is a beautiful day," added Pearl.

Is no one on my side? thought Lani, trying to think of a polite way out. Trapped in a small boat in the middle of Hāna Bay with Easton wasn't exactly her idea of an enjoyable afternoon. Fishing was supposed to be peaceful and relaxing, but with Easton seated across from her, there would be no peace or relaxation. Every glance he directed her way caused her anxiety. And yet how could she get out of it now, with Puna pulling the rug out from under her excuses?

"You did throw an omelet on my lap this morning," reminded Easton. "This can be your way of making it up to me."

"I made you oatmeal to make it up to you."

"No. You made me oatmeal because this is a bed and *breakfast*," he countered.

Out of excuses, ideas, and patience, Lani sighed. "Okay. Give me thirty minutes to clean up breakfast and get changed, and I'll meet you by the shed."

His grin bordered on triumphant. "Thirty minutes it is."

As Lani fled once more to the kitchen, she got the impression that Easton didn't really need to go fishing anymore. He'd already caught what he wanted.

She purposefully took her time cleaning and changing, and nearly an hour later she finally wandered out to the shed, hoping Easton had given up on her.

He hadn't.

Easton drove the oars hard into the water and pulled, wanting to chant, *Heave ho, and off we go.* Unfortunately, the boat didn't exactly glide through the water. Clouds had rolled in and the wind had kicked up, making the bay fairly choppy. And because it happened to be a popular snorkeling spot, they needed to row pretty far out to avoid all the swimmers, along with the few people who were trying their hand at shore fishing.

Lani sat at the tip of the boat, as far from Easton as she could possibly get, and kept her focus trained on the water. She wore a fitted t-shirt, shorts, and a wide-brimmed sun hat with her hair loose around her face, flapping in the breeze. She looked beautiful and . . . stiff, her body language screaming that this was the last place she wanted to be—or rather, that Easton was the last person she wanted to be with. Too bad for her that Cora and Pearl hadn't felt the same.

Easton hid a smile.

After the potluck, he'd kept his distance for a few days, content to spend some alone-time hiking and exploring, searching for something unique and off the beaten path. But when he came up with nada, he finally took a break and hit a few of the more impressive tourist sites like the Seven Sacred Pools and the Pipiwai Trail. Like the guidebooks touted, they were impressive, but useless to him.

The truth was he needed Lani. And even though he tried to convince himself that was the only reason he wanted to pursue her, deep inside, he knew it was more than that. He felt the way a fish might as it stared at a hook with the most tempting bait it had ever seen, and Easton didn't know if he had it in him to swim away. When this morning had presented him with the perfect opportunity to take Pearl's suggestion, he caved and nibbled.

"Tell me about your family," Easton said as he drove the oars into the water yet again.

The question earned him a brief glance in his direction. "Not much to say. My parents divorced years ago. My dad is constantly on the road as a motivational speaker. He always sends me a Christmas card and occasionally remembers my birthday. My mother owns a yoga studio in Carlsbad that keeps her incredibly busy, and she rarely calls, but she always remembers to send a gift for my birthday." She pointed to her hat as an example. "My two brothers are pretty absent as well, living in the East and Midwest with families of their own now."

She said it all in an unemotional, robotic way, but her eyes told him a different story. Her family's lack of closeness bothered her. And why wouldn't it? It bothered Easton. After watching her interact with her grandmother, he'd assumed that's how things rolled with the rest of her family. Families were cornerstones of the Hawaiian culture, after all, and Lani was awesome. What sort of parents wouldn't want to maintain a close relationship with her?

At least Cora had better sense.

"What about your family?" Lani asked. "Do your parents live in Boston?"

"Not *in* Boston. Just outside, in Ashland. My three sisters and their families live within thirty minutes of them."

"Is your family close?"

Easton hesitated, not wanting to rub in the fact that he had a close-knit family while she didn't. But he didn't want to lie either. "Yeah," he finally said. "We're close. At least the rest of them are. I'm in Hāna at the moment, which . . . isn't close—to anything, as it turns out. Not when I have to drive ninety minutes just to buy a door lock."

She smiled softly. "It's close to the sea and the mountains and incredible beauty."

"Agreed," he said. "And California's close to the sea and mountains and incredible beauty too, right?"

Her smile wilted a little. "I guess. It's just . . . busier there. More rushed, you know?"

"I do know. Boston isn't exactly rural."

"No, I guess not." She dipped her hand in the water and let it move with the rhythm of the ocean, almost as though she could sense the rises and falls.

Easton couldn't help but ask, "You're obviously not a fan of California, so why move back?"

"Because I want to."

"Really?"

She avoided eye contact. "Yes. And stop trying to change the subject."

"Change it from what?"

"Your family."

"Oh." Easton had thought they were finished with that subject. "What else do you want to know about them?"

"Do you have any nieces? Nephews?"

"Five." His arms were aching, so he lowered the oars to his lap and gave his muscles a break. "One spoiled-rotten girl and four hyperactive boys."

She cocked her head to the side and peered at him. "Do you see them much?"

He nodded, thinking back to when he last saw everyone. "That's where I go between my trips, which usually turns out to be about five times a year."

"And everyone gets together when you're in town?"

"When I'm in town, when I'm not in town. They get together all the time. My mom always hosts Sunday dinners, and then there are birthdays to celebrate, special occasions, and just-because-my-mom-happened-to-cook-an-extra-ham get-togethers. When I'm home, it's an endless sea of dinners, day trips, games, and volleyball tournaments—when the weather's good, anyway. And then there's—"

Easton stopped short when he saw the expression on Lani's face—the one that said *I'm trying really hard to be happy for you, but this is hard to hear.* He'd gotten carried away, and he inwardly kicked himself for it.

"And then there's what?" she asked.

He'd been going to say the Red Sox, Celtics, Bruins, and Patriots games, but he'd shove a raw fish in his mouth before he admitted that.

"Nothing," he said instead. "Sorry. I don't usually go off about my family like that." He squinted across the ocean. They were far enough from land that only the occasional squeal or yell could be heard from those hanging out on the beach.

She sighed and leaned forward, looking him in the eye.

"You don't have to apologize for having a wonderful family. It's nice hearing you talk, and you should brag about them." She smiled. "I brag about Puna all the time."

Easton picked up the oars and began rowing again. A little farther and they should be in a good place to fish. "Have you and your grandma always been close?"

She sat back and let her hand continue to play in the water. "No. When my dad wasn't traveling for work, he didn't want to go anywhere, and my mom was never interested in coming to visit. She fell in love with the hustle and bustle of California and can't stand not being busy. Puna and my grandfather came to visit us a few times when I was young, but only briefly, so I never got to know them well."

"What brought you here?" Easton asked, genuinely interested.

"About five years ago, Ahe's mother called, explaining that Puna's knees were giving her so much pain she could hardly get around, and she refused to go to the doctor. I think she was hoping my mother could talk some sense into her."

"I take it she did?" From what Easton had seen, Cora got around just fine—no limping or favoring of either of her knees.

"Oh, my mom called and tried to talk to her, but Puna wouldn't listen to her either."

Easton suddenly felt like he was in the middle of a really good book that he couldn't put down. He stopped rowing again and leaned forward. "So what happened?"

Lani shrugged. "I offered to come and stay with her for a while. Since my grandfather had already passed away, I figured she probably didn't want to put anyone out and that's why she was being so stubborn about it. And I was right. She fought me for a few weeks, but I scheduled the appointment anyway and booked a flight to Honolulu to see the doctor. She grudgingly came along and discovered she had no cartilage left in either of her knees. Three weeks later, after I convinced her I wasn't going anywhere until she was back on her feet, she had her first knee replacement surgery. Her recovery was rough, so she put off the second surgery until she couldn't bear to walk on the other knee anymore, and about two years after her first, she had the second. And just like I promised, I stayed until she was back on her feet and then some." She laughed softly. "What can I say? Puna and Hāna grew on me pretty quick."

Just like Lani was growing on him.

Easton's mouth felt dry, so he swallowed. Then swallowed again and even cleared his throat. If the situation had been reversed, and an estranged grandparent had needed his help, would he have done the same? Easton couldn't say that he would have. The more he got to know Lani, the more he wanted to keep getting to know her. Her beauty went far deeper than her chocolate eyes, flawless skin, and attractive curves. It came from her soul. She was a good person.

"I think we're far enough out if you're still inclined to fish," she said.

Grateful to be done with rowing for a while, Easton tucked the oars into the boat and rubbed his hands together. "Where do we start?"

She paused with her hands about to open the tackle box and arched an eyebrow. "I assumed you were a seasoned fisherman since you *love* fishing so much."

He chuckled. "I'm loving it today."

Her response was to pry open the tackle box as quickly as possible. She fished out a hook and sinkers and handed them to him. "Tie those on your line, and we'll see if the fish are interested in brown shrimp today."

Easton did as she asked, then shoved a small shrimp on the end. "Now what?"

She pointed to his pole. "Put your thumb there, flip that lever, and let go of the line as you cast. Surely you've been fishing before."

"What lever?" he asked, avoiding her question. Yes, he'd fished before and knew what lever she was talking about, but if he admitted that, there wouldn't be a reason for her to move a little closer to point it out to him. Which she did.

"That lever," she said, sitting on the bench seat next to him.

"And my thumb goes where? Here?" He put his thumb in the wrong spot, and stifled a smile when her fingers picked it up, pulled at the line, and set it down where it needed to be. All those chick flicks his sisters used to make him watch were paying off.

"Now stop pretending to be ignorant and cast, will you?" she said.

He grinned as he tossed the hook far out into the sea. She'd voluntarily touched him despite the fact that she'd seen through his pathetic antics. That had to be a good sign.

Slowly, he began to reel the line back in, wondering if they'd catch anything worth eating or anything at all. Knowing his luck, he'd snag a character from Nemo—hopefully not one of the blood-thirsty ones.

"Do sharks like brown shrimp?" he asked.

"Love them," she said, without even a hint of a smile.

"You're joking."

"Nope."

His mouth was beginning to hurt from all the smiling he'd done today, so he straightened it out and returned his attention to the line. "Here, fishy-fishy," he called. "Give that shrimp a try so Lani can have a reason to go back to work instead of enjoying this beautiful, overcast day with me."

As if in answer to his plea, the line gave a hard jerk, tugging the pole—and Easton—with it.

chapter 9

Easton would have toppled out of the boat if Lani hadn't launched forward and grabbed him around the waist. The boat rocked precariously, splashing him in the face with sea water. He tried to push the trigger to release the line, but it wouldn't budge.

"Should I let go? I can't release the line," he said, not that he'd have much of a choice in a minute. The handle was beginning to slip.

"No!" she said. "That pole is my grandfather's. It would break Puna's heart if we lost it. Can you reel it in at all?"

"Not in this position." Slowly, Easton tightened his grip and began to inch his way backwards. His fingers were beginning to cramp, but he continued to fight for Cora's sake. He didn't want to be responsible for losing a sentimental fishing pole.

Lani's arms continued to hold him around his waist until he was far enough in, then she grabbed the handle above his fingers, making it easier to hold the pole. With her help, he managed to get a better grip and adjust positions enough so that he could brace his legs against the side of the boat.

"Want me to cut the line?" Lani asked, still snug against him and holding on with both hands.

"Do you think we caught a fish, or some sort of heavy object?"

"How could a heavy object nearly pull you from the boat?"

She made a good point. It was strange. Although the pole was nearly bent in half and jostled with the movements of the water, it didn't fling about like something large and ornery was putting up a fight. Nor was the boat being pulled in the direction of the line. It was like a large boulder had fallen from the sky, caught the hook on its way down, and now held it steady.

"Am I even helping?" she asked.

Her touch was definitely helping. Where her arms tangled with his, his skin felt charged and sensitive. Every adjustment she made, he noticed—from the contour of her curves to the chill of her fingers.

The worst of the weight seemed to ease up a little, and Easton tried turning the reel again. Surprisingly, the spinner began to rotate, the line began to move, and whatever they'd caught seemed to move with it.

"Do you still need me to hold it?" Lani asked, probably anxious to get away from him.

The devil inside Easton had him saying, "If you let go and I start getting pulled out of the boat again, I'm not going to care too much that this is your grandfather's pole."

She tightened her hold and scooted even closer. And then the rod began to jerk and tug like the fish had finally decided to fight back.

Easton's curiosity overtook him, and he continued to reel it in, faster now. When he finally caught sight of movement, he squinted at what appeared to be an average-sized fish, almost like a large trout. Seconds later it broke the surface, revealing an ugly gray—pathetically small—fish about five inches from head to tail.

For a second, he and Lani glanced at each other, her expression as confused as his probably looked. Then she immediately let go and scrambled away from him, appearing more angry than confused.

She gestured toward the fish. "Wow, that's massive. I can see why it took so much effort to reel in." Her voice held a large amount of sarcasm—the accusing kind.

"This isn't what I caught," said Easton, realizing how stupid it sounded the moment the words left his mouth. "I mean, you saw the rod, it was practically bent in half."

"I was too up close and personal with the back of your shoulder to see anything."

"You had to have felt it," he argued. "And you saw me almost get pulled out of the boat."

"I'm beginning to think that what I saw was a show."

"Give me a break. Something must have happened because it felt like I was reeling in at least a thirty-pounder."

"So what, a bigger fish swallowed this one, then let it go at the last second?" she asked, her voice still miffed.

Easton kept his mouth shut, knowing further arguing would be useless. The fish still fought for its life on the hook, so he quickly grabbed it, pried the hook from its mouth, and tossed it back into the ocean.

"You know what I think?" said Lani.

He tossed the fishing pole on the bottom of the boat and grudgingly met Lani's gaze. Based on the sizzle in her eyes and the firm set of her jaw, he could venture a pretty good guess.

"I think you get a kick out of flirting. I think that most girls fall for your handsome smile and suave charm, and when you come across one who doesn't, it only makes her that much more of a challenge, and heaven forbid you back down. Am I right? How many other girls have there been? Did you leave one in China? The Azores? What about Europe and Australia?

Easton remained quiet, but he had to wonder about the root of this outburst. From day one, he'd flirted and teased and pushed the boundaries, so what about today had made her crack? Lani was flat-out ticked.

And apparently, she wasn't finished. "What are you trying to do, anyway? Make me fall for you so I'll dump a guy who's been loyal and good to me for nine years? And for what? So you can have your fun and walk away at the end of the summer? Do you really think that's okay? I am *not* a toy you can mess around with then toss to the side when you get bored. I am a human being with a heart, feelings, and a soul. Do you have any idea why I love Hāna so much? Because relationships here are forever. Friends become family and family becomes people you care about the rest of your life, and *those* are the only kinds of relationships I want. So you can take any ideas you might still have about messing with me and drown them, okay? I am not about to give up a good man and the promise of a long-lasting relationship for a few months of fun with you."

When he didn't answer right away, her rigid posture slackened, and she dropped her head to her hands. "Please," she said, looking more vulnerable than he'd imagined her capable of. "Just stop."

Easton watched her, feeling like he was back in the car

with Samah, getting raked over the coals yet again. Only this time, the guilt ran deeper—no, it was more than that. The sense of loss ran deeper. Easton had begun to wonder what it'd be like to have the sort of relationship she'd talked about with a woman—not anytime soon, but . . . someday. But now it felt like that futuristic woman had a name, an alluring body with a caring heart, quick mind, and a strong stubborn streak.

I hope she breaks your heart.

Samah's words thudded in his brain, and for the first time in his life, Easton wondered if his heart was susceptible to breaking and if Lani would be the one to fulfill Samah's wish. He couldn't deny that the thought of walking away from Lani would bother him, but did he feel this way, as she suggested, because he didn't like to lose, or was it something more?

That, he didn't know.

The good, selfless person would lick his wounds and do as she asked, but Easton had always been more selfish than not-selfish, and since he didn't want to let go just yet, he wasn't sure if he could.

What he could do was take her home.

He leaned forward to grab the oars then thrust them into the water and began the arduous journey back to the dock.

The moment the truck stopped in the drive, Lani fished the keys from the ignition and jumped out, speeding past Puna, who was pruning the bushes. She left the boat in the back of the truck, didn't bother putting the fishing gear away, and didn't even glance Easton's way. She had to get away from him and the sooner the better.

Once inside, she let the screen door slam behind her then ran to her room where she closed the door and leaned against it, gulping in huge breaths of air. Her entire body shook as she lowered herself to the ground and hugged her knees close while every ounce of self-preservation screamed at her to get on the first flight out of Maui and fly as far from Easton as possible.

Only where would she go?

After today's revelation, California was no longer an option.

Lani dropped her head between her knees as a renewed wave of heaviness hit her. It had happened so fast, yet gradually at the same time—gradual enough that Lani didn't realize she was in over her head until it was too late. That moment came when she sat in the boat, plastered to Easton's side. One sensation after another poured over her like the break of a wave, making her feel more alive than she'd ever felt with Derek. Like bursts of lightning, the revelations had come. Easton making her smile and laugh, catching her eye every time he moved and making her wonder about the world outside of Hāna. His kindness to her grandmother, the way he talked about his family, the way she'd clung to him like she'd never clung to anyone, wanting to do more than cling . . . it had culminated into one sickening and enlightening thought.

I can't marry Derek—not when I feel this way about someone else.

Then Easton had reeled in that tiny little fish, and another wave of realization came. It had all been a ploy. Everything about him was a ploy. He didn't care about anyone but himself. Once the prize was won, the game would be over, and everyone but Easton would lose.

A knock sounded, and the door vibrated behind her back.

"Lani?" came Puna's voice.

Lani drew in a shuddering breath and tried to force some energy back into her body. She needed to get moving and forget about this morning. If she could shake it off, maybe she wouldn't feel the driving need to flee the island and go who knows where.

"Can I come in?"

Lani scooted to the side and rested her head against the wall, wondering how she was supposed to explain her pathetic state to her grandmother.

But she didn't have to. Puna walked in, took one look at her, and her expression became sympathetic. "You finally know, don't you?"

"Know what?" said Lani, too shaken to figure out what she apparently already knew.

"What it feels like to soar."

The words caught her off guard, but Lani immediately dismissed them. Soaring was supposed to be freeing, exciting, thrilling—not sickening. No, what Lani was feeling was more like a splat.

Five years Derek had waited for her to come back. *Five years.* After all this time—after all his goodness—how could she bring herself to tell him that all those years of dating and waiting had really been wasted?

She couldn't.

"Puna, what am I going to do?" Her head felt heavy and cluttered, like an attic jam-packed with a bunch of stuff she had no desire to sort through.

Her grandmother picked up her hand and set something hard, cool, and rectangular on her palm. A cell phone. She closed Lani's fingers around it and said, "When you're ready, you start by calling Derek, so he can move on with his life while you move on with yours. That's what you do."

Lani stared at the phone for a full minute. "How do I tell him he's wasted all those years?"

Puna placed her hand alongside Lani's cheek, forcing her to look up. "Derek has taught you much, and you have taught him much. The two of you have developed a strong friendship—one that can last beyond this if you'll allow it. That kind of time is never wasted." Puna patted her cheek. "Cheer up, *mea aloha*. Derek will be okay, and everything will work out in the end. It always does."

After her grandmother left, Lani stared at the phone, trying to think of the right words to say. When nothing came to mind, she finally forced her fingers to dial his number anyway. Then she drew in a deep breath and waited for him to answer.

Please be able to forgive me for this, she thought as it rang.

"Hey, Lani," his deep, mellow voice answered right away. "This is a nice surprise. You don't usually call so early." It was just after five in the evening his time.

A lump the size of Jupiter formed in Lani's throat. She tried to swallow it, but it wouldn't budge.

"Lani? You there?"

"I'm here," she finally croaked in barely a whisper.

"Is everything okay?"

A heaviness filled the silence the way sand filled an hourglass, in a steady stream, flowing down and expanding until there was no more room for anything but the truth.

"Derek, I haven't been fair to you."

A stoic silence met her awkward apologies and explanations, her pleas for his forgiveness. She droned on, filling the gaps and crevices with more and more words—empty words, painful words. And when nothing more could be said, she ended the only way she could.

"I'm so sorry."

He didn't answer right away, and when he did, his voice was sad—sadder than she'd ever heard it. "I'm sorry, too. But if I'm being honest, I'm not surprised. Deep down, I knew. I just couldn't make myself believe that you didn't love me."

"I do love you, Derek." If nothing else, he needed to understand that.

"I know," he said. "Just not enough."

Lani had no reply for that. *You deserve better* or *There's someone out there more right for you than me* sounded trite and weak, even though both were true.

"Will we stay friends?" she said quietly, knowing it was too soon to ask, too soon to hope.

He let out a deep breath. "I hope so. Eventually."

She nodded even though he couldn't see her. It hurt, losing him.

"Take care of yourself, Lani." He was ready to end the conversation, and she couldn't blame him. But hanging up seemed so final, so . . . done. She wasn't prepared to be done with him, not yet. Why couldn't they have started off as friends and remained friends? Why had she let it become a romance? Romance was like walking a tightrope towards someone else. If you actually made it to the other side, you were lucky. If you wobbled and shook and fell, so long to that person forever.

Forever was a long time to not hear Derek's voice or see his smile or feel the comfort that always came from one of his hugs.

"You take care too, Derek," she forced the words out, and as soon as she said them, the line went dead.

Lani actually liked that he hadn't said goodbye. It gave her reason to hope that maybe, someday, they could be friends again.

chapter 10

F or three entire days, Lani managed to avoid Easton. She let Puna serve breakfast and took over the indoor duties. She scrubbed floors on her hands and knees, polished and dusted every frame, light fixture, and blind, and even oiled the chopping block in the kitchen. Their home and office had never looked—or smelled—so good.

If she had to run an errand or needed to get away, she'd peek out the window, make sure Easton was nowhere in sight, then make a beeline for the truck. She'd drive to town or meet up with Ahe and her other friends somewhere. On the third day, when she couldn't find anything else to clean, she bumped up the monthly Costco run by a week and drove the dreaded Hāna Highway. She rolled down her windows, let the fresh air clear her mind, ignored all the curves of the road, and enjoyed the scenery like she hadn't since the first time she'd traveled to Hāna.

If there was a positive to Easton's disruption of her life, it was this. He'd given her the freedom to remain in Hāna indefinitely, and she was grudgingly grateful for that. She just needed him to leave so that life could get back to normal.

On Wednesday morning Lani awoke before the sun. After tossing and turning and trying to lull herself back to sleep, she threw the covers off and paced her room. Then she paced the front room. When the walls began encroaching on her, she went out to the lanai and watched the horizon turn from a grayish haze to a light pink. As soon as Easton's bungalow became visible, she walked back inside, left Puna a note asking her to serve the muffins, fruit, and juice she'd prepared the night before, and quickly dressed.

What she needed most was a day trip to Kapu Aina, her favorite spot on the island, but it wasn't a good hike to take in the rain, and with the looming clouds, she didn't dare risk it. So she dragged her bike from the shed instead, added air to the tires, and rode south on Hāna Highway during one of the few times of day when the road wasn't lined with tourists. She made it about a mile when the sun's belly began to rise above the ocean. Stopping for a few moments to admire the view, Lani felt at peace for the first time since she'd opened her eyes that morning.

She watched a car pass, then hopped back on her bike and continued south. She didn't stop until she arrived at the Pools of 'Ohe'o. This was the only time of day Lani ever ventured here; the only time when it wasn't bustling with people and voices and cameras. Most locals stayed away completely, but Lani loved walking the grounds, dipping her feet in the pools, and even hiking the Pipiwai trail when only the clack of the bamboo trees could be heard.

Despite the overcast skies, the gates to the pools were open, so she wandered down, slipped off her sandals, and soaked her feet. The Seven Sacred Pools was a name invented a few decades earlier as a marketing ploy to draw more tourists to this area, so she didn't place much stock in the name. But during moments like this when Lani was surrounded by the beauty of the rocks, water, lushness, with the landscape of the ocean before her, it felt sacred.

She relaxed against a smooth rock and closed her eyes, letting the serenity and rising sun warm her body. She even fell asleep for a time—until engines and tires scrunching against asphalt awoke her from dreams of two men walking away from her—Easton going one way and Derek another.

When voices in the distance grew louder, Lani pulled her feet from the water, pushed her feet back into her sandals, and trotted up the stairs to retrieve her bike. Soon she was riding north on Hāna Highway while most of the cars traveled south.

About a hundred yards or so up the road, her tire blew. It went from inflated to deflated in a second, forcing her to skid to an awkward and bumpy stop. Seconds later, a raindrop landed on her nose, followed by another on her cheek and several on her arms. Lani looked up at the sky as the clouds let loose, and the light sprinkle became a gushing torrent.

Lani glanced longingly up the road, knowing she was stranded for now. If she left her bike behind and tried to walk home, it would be an accident waiting to happen. No car would be able to see her in this mess. Across the street there was a wider shoulder near a large tree, so she waited for another car to zip past then ran her bike to the spot, where she could wait out the worst of the rain with whatever shelter the tree provided.

Once there, Lani plopped down on a small lava rock and watched the rain come.

"Aloha, Cora. Pearl," Easton trotted up the lanai's steps to get out of the rain. Once under the protection of the tin roof, he brushed the collected drops from his arms and shook his Red Sox hat off before putting it back on. He had to raise his voice to be heard above the pounding.

"So much for that hike I was going to take this morning."

"Hiking would be a mucky mess in this weather," agreed Cora with a smile. "Did you sleep well?"

"Yes." At least as well as someone could sleep on the awful mattress in the bungalow, though compared to some of the places he'd slept over the years, it was still a solid average.

"There's some food on the table over there." Cora gestured with a wave of her hand. "It's just a light breakfast this morning. I hope that's okay."

"It's perfect. Mahalo." Easton crossed the porch and glanced at the door leading into the house, hoping for a glimpse of Lani. But she was nowhere in sight, just like the past three days. Apparently when Lani wanted to avoid someone, she did it well.

He poured himself some juice then grabbed a muffin and a banana.

"Come join us." Pearl gestured toward the open seat next to them.

Easton did and took a swig of what tasted like a mixture of freshly squeezed orange and passion fruit juice. He liked it.

"Where were you planning to hike this morning?" asked Pearl.

"Nowhere in particular. I wanted to drive down Hāna Highway, take the first road that I could find heading west, go to the end, and see where it took me."

Cora topped off his juice. "Lani usually gives everyone a map of some of the best trails around here. Didn't she give one to you?"

"She did. I just like finding my own way, I guess you could say. Speaking of which, do you happen to know of any lesser-known trails or destinations? I'm not much of a join-the-tourist-throng sort of guy."

Cora crinkled her brows in thought for a moment before saying, "Kadir used to love to wander the hills above the property, but I wouldn't call it a destination hike. Sorry, I'm not very helpful, am I? Lani will probably know some other places. You should ask her. Or even Ahe. That group is always traipsing off somewhere."

"Good idea," said Easton, although something told him that neither Ahe nor Lani would be too forthcoming. He took a bite of his muffin and glanced at the door again, wondering where Lani was and how long it would be before she stopped avoiding him. He missed her.

"Looking for someone?" Cora asked casually—a little too casually.

Easton cleared his throat and returned his attention to the two women. "I think your internet is down. I tried bringing my laptop to the lobby a little while ago and couldn't connect to your wi-fi like I usually can. Any idea why, or if it will be working again soon?"

Cora's lips puckered into a frown, and she shook her head. "Sorry. I don't know much about that sort of stuff. You'll want to ask Lani about that as well. Or you could always go to the lobby at the Travassa and connect to theirs. Some of the staff are Lani's friends, and they're nice enough to give our guests access to their internet when ours goes down. But you'll still need to ask Lani what the password is because I can't remember."

Easton would love to ask Lani about the password. He'd love to ask her a lot of things, such as when she was planning on talking to him again. "Any idea where I could find her this morning?"

Cora offered him a rueful smile. "Wish I could, but she was up before me today again. Left a note saying she had a few things to do and would be back later this morning. I'm sure she'll show up any moment now." She didn't look too convinced.

"Would she have taken the truck?" Easton asked.

"Considering it's our only car, I'm sure she did."

"Then she's got to be around here somewhere. I saw your truck out front on my way down—the same place it was parked an hour ago when I tried using the internet in the lobby."

"Really?" Cora frowned. "I haven't seen her at all. It's not like she'd go walking off in this weather."

Pearl slowly raised her cup of cocoa to her lips, but not before Easton saw a hint of a smile. When she was done sipping, she said, "I heard some noise coming from the shed early this morning. Is there some other mode of transportation she might have taken?"

Cora's frown became an expression of concern. "Oh dear," she said, sliding her chair back. "She probably went for a bike ride and is soaked to the bone right now. I'd better go find her."

Before she could stand, Easton set his cup down and hopped to his feet. "Why don't you let me go? I'm already wet and need to talk to her anyway. Any idea which way she might have gone?"

"That would be wonderful," said Cora. "Mahalo, Easton. Some mornings she likes to ride to the Pools at 'Ohe'o, but . . . yes, I would bet my knitting needles that's where she went. Do you know where 'Ohe'o is?"

"I was there last week. I'll see if I can find her."

Cora touched his arm. "Her bike is neon pink. Ahe made her paint it that color so she'd be seen easily."

Easton hid a smile and jogged down the steps again, into what was now a light shower. Two minutes later, he was in his rented Subaru, driving south on the Hāna Highway. Fifteen minutes after that, the rain had become a sprinkle, and he finally spotted a neon pink bike being pushed by a woman with dark, wet hair and clothes plastered to a beautiful, slender body with curves in all the right places. His heart beat a little quicker at the sight.

He immediately pulled to the side of the road and got out of his car. Lani had stopped walking and was looking at him—or, more specifically, his car.

"You're looking a little soggy," he said. "Want a ride?"

Her expression was one of indecision before she said, "No. I'm good." She continued pushing her bike, the front tire completely flat.

"You sure?"

"Yep."

He glanced at his watch to check the time. "It took me about fifteen minutes to drive here, which means, at the rate you're walking, it will probably take you about an hour to get home." He paused, letting his words sink in before adding, "Still sure you don't want a lift? In fifteen minutes, you can be in a nice, hot shower."

She continued to trudge along, her movements determined. When her front tire dropped into a puddle and splashed muddy water up her legs, her jaw clenched.

Easton hid a smile and tried a different tactic. "Your grandma is worried about you."

Apparently that was the golden ticket because Lani hesitated, then looked over her shoulder. "Okay, you win. I'd love a ride."

"Even if it's with me?" he asked.

"Even with you." She sounded resigned, but turned her bike around and began pushing it his way. Easton jogged across the street and took it from her, carrying it back to the car. It took folding down the back seats and taking off the front tire, but they were finally able to get it inside.

"Mahalo," she said, once they were out of the drizzle and back in the car. Easton slid the key into the ignition but left it there, twisting toward her and resting his elbow on the steering wheel instead. "I think you've been avoiding me."

She stared out the dashboard window, her palms rubbing together like she was cold. "What is it you want from me?"

Easton started the car and turned up the heat. Then he chewed on the inside of his cheek, trying to figure out what he *did* want. Yes, he'd like access to her knowledge of the land and her understanding of local ways, but he also missed seeing her, talking to her, making her lips strain whenever she tried not to smile, or watching her emotions play across her face like a movie screen.

"I want to be your friend," he finally said, cringing inwardly at how cliché it sounded. Heart-to-hearts weren't exactly his style. They made him uncomfortable, just like goodbyes, define-the-relationship talks, and confrontations made him uncomfortable, or pretty much any conversation involving the need for him to share his innermost thoughts and feelings. Easton preferred lighter topics.

But lighter wasn't going to get him anywhere with Lani.

"I'm not sure you're capable of being friends with a woman," she said.

"I'm friends with Pearl and your grandmother."

"You know what I mean."

In the rearview mirror, a silver SUV grew closer then

passed. A kid had his head out the window and was flapping his arms wildly in the air, looking like he was having the time of his life. Part of Easton wished that he could hitch a ride, so he could get away from the expression in Lani's eyes that said, *I need you to be serious and tell me what you're really thinking.*

In other words, if he couldn't come up with something, he might as well take her home and plan to stay out of her way the rest of the summer.

Easton continued watching the SUV until it disappeared from sight. Then he drew in a deep breath and forced the words out. "I'm not going to deny that I'm attracted to you, or that I want to keep spending time with you. But I'm truly sorry for making you uncomfortable by not respecting your relationship with that guy in California—"

"Derek," she said.

"Yes, him. And . . . I guess what I'm saying is that I'd rather be your friend than nothing."

"Derek and I aren't together anymore," she said quietly—too quietly. Easton wasn't sure if he'd heard right.

"Puna has been trying to tell me we weren't right for each other, but I didn't want to believe it. So I agreed to move back and marry him at the end of the summer, only . . . I can't—not when I've felt more and more unsettled with each passing day. So . . . we're not together."

The car suddenly felt like a sauna, so Easton cracked the window. He hadn't expected this. Had she broken up with Derek because of him? Did her feelings run deeper than she'd let on? Was she wanting—

"Your head is swelling by the second," said Lani.

"What?"

"Believe it or not, this isn't about you. It's about me finally figuring out that I could never make Derek happy and feeling horrible for letting our relationship drag out for so long. The only reason I'm telling you is because I don't want you to feel guilty either. Apparently you saw what Puna, and even Pearl, saw. I was just blind, I guess."

Easton should correct her. He should tell her he hadn't seen any writing on any wall. The only thing he'd seen was an intriguing and beautiful woman who wasn't wearing a ring on the fourth finger of her left hand.

But he didn't.

"We still need to get something straight," she continued. "In a few months, you'll be leaving. And even though I'm technically free now, I'm still not interested in a short-term relationship with you or anyone else. So if you think you're capable of friendship, great. If not, I need you to keep your distance, and I'll keep . . . keeping mine."

Easton bit down on his lower lip. He wanted to argue the merits of short-term relationships. No expectations, no DTRs, no stress about the future. Just live-in-the-moment fun. Even Samah had been fine with it. Her beef had come from him leaving without a goodbye.

But he didn't do that either. Something told him Lani wouldn't see things his way.

Several cars zipped past, and Easton continued to watch in the mirror as they rounded the bend behind them, choosing his words carefully. "You're right in thinking I might not be capable of friendship. But I *know* I'm not capable of keeping my distance, so . . . friends?"

She snickered then shook her head as she looked out the window. "At least you're honest about it. Just promise you'll tone the flirting way down, okay?"

"I can't even flirt with you?" Even friends flirted with each other on occasion, didn't they?

"Please, Easton." All traces of humor gone, her voice

was a quiet plea, an honest plea. One that said, *Don't break my heart.*

In that moment, Easton finally understood. She *did* have feelings for him. Maybe her breakup with Derek hadn't been all about him, but part of it had been. And if that was the case, then a third option existed. An implied option. She said she wasn't interested in a short-term relationship, but had said nothing about long-term. In other words, if he was going to play the game, he'd better be playing for keeps.

Easton suddenly felt weighted down with a responsibility he didn't want. It changed things, made them more serious. But he wasn't ready to think beyond summer and into the future or even move forward with that as a possibility. So when it came down to it, he really did only have two options.

Friendship or distance.

The once-refreshing overcast skies turned gloomy and dank. Despite the light sprinkle, Easton rolled his window all the way down and drew in a deep breath. He glanced over his shoulder to wait for a break in traffic, and as soon as he could, pulled out onto the highway.

chapter 11

Easton ran a screwdriver underneath the rim of the bike tire, then pried it up so he could remove the flattened tube. He wasn't sure why he'd insisted on fixing Lani's tire for her, but he had.

"I'll fix it," he'd said.

"Please don't worry about it."

"It's not a problem."

"Yes it is," she insisted. "Those brakes are a pain to get off."

"Which is why you should be thanking me instead of arguing."

Things had escalated from there, turning into a full-blown argument before she'd finally thrown her hands into the air and said, "Fine. If you want to waste your vacation fixing a flat, feel free."

No mahalo. No nothing. Just frustrated movements as she stalked away, leaving Easton with his stubborn pride, a

111

neon pink bike, and a disorganized shed. It took him nearly thirty minutes to find a patch kit.

Only then had he paused to consider his motives or whether or not he needed his head examined. Easton hated fixing bike tires almost as much as he hated serious conversations. Yet here he stood, wrestling a flimsy tube from a stiff, rubber tire.

Why did he care so much? Why couldn't he forget Lani, focus on what needed to be done, and go his merry way? That would be so much easier and less complicated.

Maybe Lani was right. Maybe this was a game to him— one that he'd never lost and couldn't stomach losing now. Maybe all he really wanted was to prove he could get the girl and the fun would be over.

Or would it?

He had no idea. His thoughts were all over the place, his emotions almost foreign. All he knew for sure is that no female had ever driven him to verbally duke it out over a twenty-six-inch bike tire.

His fingers ran along the inside of the rubber, searching for the source of the flat. When he found no thorns or nails, he filled the tube with air and hunted for holes. Still no luck, which was strange. The tire had been completely flat—not sort of flat, *completely* flat. That typically meant a large thorn or nail had forced its way through. It should be whistling and wheezing right now.

Cursing himself for having to deal with this, Easton stalked up the hill to the bungalow, filled his sink with water, and slowly pushed the tube through the bath, watching for air bubbles. When none surfaced, he pulled the tube from the sink and frowned.

Then it hit him. Maybe the reason that Lani had been so opposed to him fixing the flat was because she knew it didn't need fixing. She'd let the air out on purpose.

But why? It didn't make any sense.

Maybe she'd known her grandmother would worry about the rain and there would be a good chance Easton would come to get her. Maybe all the "avoiding" she'd been doing over the past three days had been her way of playing hard to get, and this was an additional ploy at attention.

It sounded way out of character and ludicrous, but what other explanation was there? Easton held the proof that someone had tampered with the tire, and who else but Lani?

Clutching the still-full tire, he trotted back down to the main house, where he found Lani in the office, staring at her cell phone with a perplexed look on her face. She'd changed out of her wet clothes, and her still-damp hair surrounded her face in loose waves.

She stared at Easton, though her eyes seemed lost in thought. "Would you believe the Nielsons just cancelled their room reservation? That's the fourth time this has happened. Don't you think that's strange?"

Easton had no idea what she was talking about, nor did he care. He held up the tire. "What's strange is there are no holes in this tube."

Her brow wrinkled, and she glanced from the tire to him. "What are you talking about?"

"Why did you let the air out of the tire?"

"I didn't."

"Then how do you explain that it's as full now as it was thirty minutes ago when I pumped it up?"

Lani pushed her chair back and came around the desk to inspect it herself. She played with it a moment before handing it back. "Haha, joke's on me. Now where's the real tube?"

"Right here."

"That's not possible. The tire went flat in seconds."

"Yeah, because you *deflated* it."

She gaped at him. "Why would I do that?"

"I have no idea. Maybe because you really don't want to avoid me and knew Cora would send me to come find you after it started raining."

Her jaw dropped open slightly before she recovered. "Do I look like someone who can control the weather? How was I supposed to know it would start raining?"

Easton had no ready answer. It was one of the things he hadn't thought through completely. Unless . . . He jabbed a finger at her. "You let the air out *after* it started raining."

"What?" she spluttered. "Why? So I could sit on the side of the highway and get soaked on the off chance you might drive by and rescue me? That's the most ridiculous thing anyone has ever accused me of."

"No more ridiculous than you accusing me of pretending to get pulled overboard by a one-pound fish."

Lani opened her mouth then closed it, shaking her head as though she couldn't believe this conversation was taking place. Easton couldn't believe it either.

She let out a breath and took a step closer, meeting his gaze with open honesty. "I didn't let the air out of my tire."

"And I didn't pretend to catch a whale."

For a moment they both stood in a tense, silent stand-off, so close he could almost touch her. She smelled like she'd just walked through an orchard of apples and plums and flowers. Her hair had fallen forward slightly, sweeping across her forehead and hiding one of her beautiful, telling eyes. The other held fear and uncertainty and possibly even desire.

More than anything, he wanted to push her hair back, touch her cheek and kiss her.

Would she let him? Was her heart pounding in her ears also? Did she have to fight against closing the distance between them as much as he did?

Easton didn't know how much longer he could stand still, resisting, fighting the battle to stay friends and only friends.

And then her shiny pink lips surprised him. Ever so slightly, they twitched at the corners. She clamped them together, but the edges of her eyes crinkled with humor. A half giggle, half snort escaped from her lips before she covered her mouth with her palm.

"Something funny?" he asked. Maybe he had something on his face. Smudges from the tire? He wiped the back of his hand across his cheek to be sure.

"Sorry," she said. "It just occurred to me that anyone hearing us would think we're both mental."

"I'm beginning to wonder if we are," said Easton, making her snicker again.

Finally, she held out her hand. "How about a truce? I promise to not accuse you of falsifying a fish's mass again if you promise to not accuse me of playing the damsel in distress. Trust me when I say that's the last part I'd ever play."

Easton believed her. He took her warm hand in his and squeezed it. "Friends again?"

She nodded. "Friends."

For a moment, his fingers tightened around hers. He wanted to tell her that friendship wasn't enough. He wanted to flirt with her, tease her, touch her, and kiss her. He wanted her to look at him with excitement and hope rather than possible regret.

Bells clanged as the the door burst opened, and Ahe and one of his sidekicks barreled inside, wearing board shorts. Lani whipped her hand from Easton's as though she'd been scalded and put them behind her back. Ahe's grin wilted when he noticed she had company.

At least he and Ahe seemed to have one thing in common, Easton thought dryly.

"*Howzit*, Lani?" Ahe said, apparently deciding that ignoring Easton was the best approach.

"Do you ever knock?" said Lani with an indulgent smile. She was obviously fond of her friend and didn't seem to mind the intrusion. Easton, on the other hand, wished he could wave a wand and make Ahe disappear.

"Hamoa's break is epic. You coming?"

"I thought you had to work today," said Lani.

"Nah. It's *pau Hāna* time."

"Yeah," added the friend whose name Easton couldn't remember. "You like go surf or wot?"

"You guys always think it's *pau Hāna* time if the break's good," said Lani. "But I'm stuck here for a little while. I've got a few reservations to confirm and some information packets to send out."

"Have fun with that." The sidekick slapped Ahe's arm. "*Ho, brah.* Let's go, yeah?"

Ahe ignored his friend and strode down the hallway instead, calling, "Ho, Auntie Cora!" Apparently he also knew the secret to getting Lani to ditch responsibility.

Lani was quick to lunge forward and grab his arm. "You know Puna will shoo me out of here, but then she'd be left with all the work, and you wouldn't want to do that to her, would you?"

His expression became almost petulant, to the point that Easton wouldn't be surprised if he stomped his foot. "You're killing me, Lani," he said.

"Give me two hours, and I'll meet you there."

"The break is epic *now*."

"Then what are you waiting for?" Lani nodded toward the door. "Two hours, and I'll catch up. Promise. Now outta here so I can get something done."

The friend disappeared first, and Ahe slowly backed toward the door, shooting Easton a distrustful look before pointing a finger at Lani. "Don't forget."

The bell jingled, and Ahe was gone, leaving Easton still standing in the middle of the room holding a grubby tire tube. The ocean was sounding pretty good right about now.

"The second his surfboard hits the water, *he'll* be the one to forget about me," said Lani with a smile.

Easton seriously doubted it, but he wasn't about to start another argument. He was more interested in discussing something else. "So . . . you're going surfing."

She walked back to her desk and sat down, then hit a few keys on the keyboard and stared at the monitor. "I am."

Normally, he didn't have to grovel for invites, but Lani wasn't exactly forthcoming with them. "You surf?" he asked.

"I grew up in California. Of course I surf."

"And you have your own board?"

"I do now. Ahe found me a great deal on a really nice one." Still no invite. Her fingers flew over the keyboard as she typed who knows what. Probably *Take the hint and go away, Easton. I'm not going to invite you surfing.*

He meandered forward and sat on the corner of the desk, tossing the tube in the air and catching it. "You know, I've always wanted to give surfing a try."

"Have you?"

He tossed the tire again. "To say I've surfed in Hawaii would be truly . . . *epic*," he said, lifting an eyebrow expectantly. "It's too bad I don't have a board. Or a capable *friend* who could teach me."

She flicked a glance at him before returning her attention to the computer. "Ahe teaches lessons and has a few boards he loans out. You could ask him."

Easton nearly snorted. He'd spend the day alone in a boat with a fishing pole before he'd ask Ahe for anything—especially lessons. He tucked the tire by his side and leaned low over the desk, dropping his voice. "Or you could teach me in, I don't know . . . say two hours?"

"I don't think so." Her focus remained on the computer and whatever words she continued to type.

So much for that angle. Easton pushed himself upright and spun the tire again. "Why not?"

Her fingers stilled, and she finally looked at him squarely in the eye. "You already know how to surf, don't you." It was a statement, not a question.

The airborne tube hit his hand and spun across the floor, and Easton half coughed, half laughed before he recovered. She'd seen right through him.

Time to cut his losses. "The truth?"

"Please."

Tire forgotten, Easton stood and shoved his hands into the pockets of his khaki shorts. "Yes, I know how to surf, though my skill level is average at best. I also know how to long board, do a pretty solid handstand on a paddleboard if the water is smooth, and if you give me a pair of decent fins, I can hold my own body surfing as well. Oh, and I can build the coolest sand sculpture you've ever seen. My sea turtle won second place in a contest once."

"Only second?"

"First place was a mermaid castle, and a six-year-old girl was the judge."

Lani's lips twitched and she ducked her head to the side to hide a full-on smile. And then she surprised him. "Okay, you're invited. Meet me by the shed in two hours."

"Really?" Easton hadn't expected honesty to work at all, especially not this fast.

She let out a breath and rested her palms over a stack of paperwork as she looked up at him. "I like real people, Easton. People with strengths and weaknesses, highs and lows, likes and dislikes. If you don't like to fish, say it. If you know how to surf, admit it. And if you're really interested in being my friend, then respect me enough to act like it."

A lump formed in Easton's throat as he realized something. Lani could banter and tease and volley with the best of them, but at her heart, she was truly genuine and had no patience with anyone who wasn't willing to be the same.

Every instinct told Easton to slowly back away and start hunting for another girl who wouldn't make things as hard or complicated or real. *She's not worth the effort or the exposure,* he tried to convince himself. But deep inside, Easton was beginning to think that maybe she was.

He crouched down and retrieved the tire tube from the floor before backing toward the door.

"See you in two."

The morning downpour paved the way for a glorious afternoon. Lani lay back on her surfboard and closed her eyes, feeling the sun warm her body and the rise and fall of the ocean remove the clutter from her mind. It had been too long since she'd felt this relaxed.

"Here it comes!" Ahe called from about six yards away.

Lani's legs squeezed the board, and she sat up and looked back. A large wave was beginning to form, so she prodded her board into place and paddled with slow, deliberate strokes. The water beneath her began to swell and rush backward, and a moment later, when her board lifted as the wave began to take over, Lani knew her timing had been perfect. A couple more strokes and she popped up, leaning to the left to get her board in trim.

Ahe yelled from behind, cheering her on. She crouched low, feeling the exhilaration that always came with the rush of wind, the smell of sea, and the simple fact that she was riding on top of the water. The wave curled over her, encasing her in a tunnel of greens, blues, and whites. Surfing was the only place Lani felt truly at one with the elements. You *had* to be at one with them or the ride would end in a painful surge of a crushing wave smashing you into the ocean floor.

She crouched lower, directing her board toward the open air. It grew closer and closer until she was out.

Her hands flew overhead as she shouted her enthusiasm.

An answering yelp echoed her, and Lani glanced over her shoulder to see Ahe coming off another wave, not far behind. She dropped to her knees and spun off the board into the knee-high water, then waited for Ahe to catch up. As he approached, she felt a surge of gratitude for her friend. Over the past five years, he'd taught her how to read the rhythm of the ocean, to let go, to live. Maybe that's why she'd resisted leaving. She didn't want to reverse anything in her life, only continue to move forward.

"That was one sweet ride, yeah?" Ahe said.

"You were right," Lani agreed. "The waves have been epic. Thanks for thinking of me."

"I always think of you, Lani." He said it with a teasing lilt to his voice. But the appreciation in his gaze told her a different story—one that made her worry. "Want to go again?"

She nodded toward the beach. "I'm pretty wiped, and I'm sure Easton wants to take a turn. Mind giving him a few pointers?"

He snorted. "The haole? Why you gotta bring him anyway?"

"You're not jealous are you, Ahe?"

Any other time, Lani could have easily predicted his answer. He would have laughed and said, "Who—me? Jealous? In yo dreams, *sistah.*" But today he surprised her. He kept quiet. And although a hint of a smile stayed perched on his lips, his eyes focused on Easton, and what she saw in them could definitely be termed as jealousy.

Ahe stopped walking and turned to Lani. "Auntie Cora told me 'bout Cali-boy," he said.

Lani sighed and adjusted her board so it wasn't digging into her armpit. "Don't tell me you're surprised." Ahe had always tolerated Derek, saying he was an okay haole, but no match for Lani. He never seemed to take their relationship too seriously, which probably explained why he'd never had a problem with Derek. With Easton, though, Ahe hadn't even tried to tolerate him.

"You break up with Cali-boy for this guy?" Ahe nodded toward Easton.

Lani nearly laughed, then shook her head. "No, not for that guy. Not for any guy. You were right. Puna was right. And Derek *wasn't* right—for me, that is. But I think he knew that too."

Ahe nodded, apparently content with her explanation, and as they walked up the beach again and he looked Easton's way, his expression was a little more . . . tolerant. Lani hid a smile. Ahe and his family had always looked out for Puna, and ever since Lani had come, they'd looked out for her too. They'd taught her the true meaning of *'ohana.*

When they reached Easton, Lani dropped one end of her board into the sand and gave it a pat. "You ready to give it a try? Ahe said he'd love to give you some pointers."

The expression on Ahe's face belied her words, and she fought back a smile.

Easton picked himself up, brushed the sand from his shorts, and accepted Lani's board before shooting a wary look at Ahe. "Mahalo, but I think I've got it."

That earned him a look of grudging respect from Ahe. "You surf?"

"Not like you two, but yeah. It's been a while though."

Ahe watched his friend, Paavo, catch a wave before he let out a heavy breath and gave Lani a look that said, *You owe me for this one.* "C'mon, haole. This break won't last forever."

"You're not planning to drown me, are you?"

Ahe actually laughed, as did Lani. "Nah. Not today, anyway."

Easton grabbed Lani's board and grinned. "In that case, what are we waiting for?"

The two men jogged off, and Lani sank down on her towel to watch. Ahe, tall, dark, and well-built, and Easton a little less tall, a little less dark, and a little less well-built. But as they dove into the waves and began to paddle out, she noticed that her mind, gaze, and thoughts followed Easton. It had been fun, hanging out with him today. He'd been mostly quiet, seemingly content to enjoy the sand, water, and sun, and, like he'd promised, hadn't flirted at all.

She tried to tell herself that she was glad, but truthfully, she missed it. She'd always thought the friend zone meant the safe zone, but now that her feelings went beyond friendship, she was quickly learning that when it came to Easton Allard, there was no safe zone.

chapter 12

A
s the days and weeks came and went, most of Lani's reservations about Easton went with them. He became exactly what he promised he would—her friend, and *only* her friend. He still teased, sometimes flirted, but mostly asked a lot of questions—about her life growing up, her family, her years in college, and Hawaii.

Easton was more open with her as well, telling her about Boston and his sisters, nieces, and nephews. He'd graduated with an Associate's from Boston University then decided college wasn't for him. So he'd quit and began traveling. After that, his history became more vague and spotty. What little she had gotten out of him, Lani pieced together that he'd worked a lot of odd jobs to pay for his new lifestyle, but he'd finally gotten to a point where he didn't have to do that much anymore. He'd visited almost every continent at least once, including Antarctica, and still wasn't satisfied. The way he talked about his travels, with awe and reverence, left Lani feeling like she was missing out on something incredible.

She'd spent a few hours searching Google, trying to figure out his online identity, but Easton, it seemed, was good at keeping secrets. Puna had once told her that everyone had good things about them and bad things about them, but the scale always tipped one way or the other. The trick was finding out which way it tipped—toward mostly good or mostly bad.

Despite his secrets, Lani was beginning to think that Easton was mostly good.

Lani stood on the threshold of the Hema room in shock. Two days. Those horrible, party-driven college students had only been here two days, and they'd completely trashed the room. And what was that odor? Ugh. She crossed the room to open windows and had to step over plates and Styrofoam containers with food spilling out of them, broken soda and beer bottles, couch cushions, and garbage and more garbage. And oh, that smell. Where was it coming from? One look in the bathroom and she found her answer. Someone had puked in the bathtub and had left another surprise in the toilet. She quickly flushed it and turned on the fan, then slammed the door and ran out of the room before she gagged.

She'd been expecting to find a mess, but not of this caliber. How could anyone live like this or be so disrespectful? She didn't understand it. Nor did she know how she would get this cleaned in time for the guests who were scheduled to check in later that afternoon. Puna was out visiting friends and wouldn't be back for hours, so it was up to Lani to get it done. But how? She'd need at least twenty-four hours and professional cleaning equipment to get the room even close to ready in time.

Unable to stand the stench any longer, Lani went out to the lanai and inhaled the lush, just-after-rain smell. Then she looked around at the overturned chairs and dried food and sighed. She had no choice but to try to get it ready. And she began by righting all the chairs.

"Ho, Lani!" Ahe's voice called from across the lawn. "I got mahi mahi today! Your favorite."

Lani's shoulders sagged as she looked at him. Ahe was a skilled fisherman and earned his meager living by selling his catch to Travaasa and the few other hotels near Hāna. But he always kept the best for family—Puna and Lani included. And they returned the good deed with loaves of bread—from banana and pumpkin to whole wheat and sourdough. It didn't matter what kind she made, Ahe's family loved them all.

Today, however, not even the thought of mahi mahi could cheer her up.

"That sounds great, Ahe. Mahalo." She tried to unflatten her tone, but it didn't rise to the occasion.

Ahe jogged up the steps and frowned at her. "Why the stinkface? It's mahi mahi!"

"No, it's not that." She gestured toward the open door and grimaced. "It's that."

Ahe took one look inside and his usual smile vanished. "No—*fo real*? Who did this?" he growled, slamming his right fist into the palm of his left hand. "Where are they? When I get through with them, they wish they be *maki die dead*." He started past her, apparently ready to hunt down the stupid college boys that he'd never even met.

Lani stayed him with a hand on his bicep and shook her head. When provoked, the mild-tempered Ahe could turn into a rhino, ready to trample anyone who messes with him or his family. If she let him go, he'd spend the rest of the day scouring the island until he found the reprobates and then beat all three of them within inches of their lives.

As upset as Lani was, she didn't want it to come to that. "They're long gone and not worth the effort it would take to track them down."

Ahe didn't agree. "They need to pay for this, Lani."

"They already have, in the form of a cleaning deposit. Please, let's leave it at that. I never want to see their faces again—especially not if they're broken, black and blue."

He didn't look happy about letting anyone off the hook, but he nodded out of respect to her.

"Mahalo for the fish," she said. "I really am grateful. Would you mind putting it in the fridge for me? I have new guests arriving this afternoon and have a lot of work to do before then."

"I'll find Taavatti. He works nights at Aloha and can get a carpet cleaner."

She smiled her gratitude. "I would love you forever if you did that. Tell him I'll pay him double whatever he charges."

He waved away her offer as though it annoyed him. "Taavatti's 'ohana. When you gonna learn that you don't pay 'ohana? I'll be back in a quick one." He bounded down the stairs faster than he'd come.

Lani quickly uncoiled the garden hose and turned it on, directing the less-than-powerful spray at the dried-on bits of food on the patio floor.

"Ey, haole!" Ahe's voice came again from farther away, and Lani glanced up to see that he wasn't talking to her. Ahe was yelling toward the bungalow.

"You talking to me?" came Easton's dry reply from

somewhere behind a cluster of palms. Probably the hammock—his favorite place to write.

"You the only haole I see."

"I figured," said Easton. "What's up?"

He pointed back at her. "Lani needs you. The Hema room is *pilau*."

Lani bit her tongue to keep from yelling at Ahe to shut up. As much as she appreciated him looking out for her, she didn't appreciate having Easton involved. He was a paying guest—not family and certainly not someone who should be asked to help.

Unfortunately, Easton was already on his way over. She watched him from the corner of her eye as she continued to spray the floor. He stopped at the bottom of the stairs and waited expectantly.

"Ahe said you needed me?"

"He was wrong. I'm fine."

"You look stressed."

"Really, I'm good."

He leaned his arm casually across the banister and pinned her with a stare. "Ahe instigated a conversation with me. He wouldn't have done that if it wasn't important. So spill."

Ignoring him, Lani focused on a particularly stubborn spot, rubbing it with her foot. But her flimsy flip flop was no match for the dried barbeque sauce, and when the sole bent in half, driving her toe into the hard wood, she threw the hose down in frustration, ready to burst into tears. The lanai alone would take hours to scrub clean.

Easton walked to her side and put a hand on her arm. His voice was gentle when he said, "Hey, what's wrong?" Before she could answer, he looked beyond her and his eyes widened. He slipped past, planting both palms against the doorframe as he assessed the damage.

"Are you kidding me?" he hissed, his tone sharper than she'd ever heard. Through the thin fabric of his Kelly-green t-shirt, his muscles tensed. Then his fingers balled into fists and his jaw tightened. For a moment, Lani expected an outburst like Ahe's, but he didn't say anything. His shoulders rose and fell as he drew in one steadying breath, then another.

Slowly, he turned around. A hard look glinted in his eyes, making Lani grateful his anger wasn't directed at her. One more deep breath, and he said, "Where do you keep your garbage bags?"

"No. You're not going to—"

"Where. Do you keep. Your garbage bags?" Apparently, he meant business and wouldn't take no for an answer.

Lani pointed around the side of the house. "There's a supply closet over there. I've already unlocked it."

Without saying anything, he walked over and pulled a few garbage bags from a box, tugged on some white Latex gloves and strode past her into the room. He didn't even complain about the smell, just got to work.

Lani located a scrub brush and dropped down on her knees, attacking the wood floor with gusto. The dried food had absorbed some of the water, making it clean up a little quicker. By the time she'd finished with the lanai and loaded a bucket with cleaning supplies from the closet, Easton had filled two bags with garbage and another with soiled towels and bed linens. He'd also put a load in the washing machine and was busy scrubbing the kitchen sink with his back to her. The room even smelled a little better.

From the doorway, Lani felt the first glimmer of hope that they could get it ready in time. As she watched Easton, a lump lodged in her throat and warmth radiated from her heart. Never before had a man looked more attractive than

Easton did at that moment. Unable to resist the impulse, Lani set her bucket down and came up behind him, wrapping her arms around his waist.

"Mahalo," she whispered, touching her cheek to his shoulder blade.

Easton's movements stilled, making Lani worry she'd crossed a line she shouldn't have. She began to pull away, but his hand covered hers, keeping her there. An outbreak of goosebumps flowed from her fingertips through the rest of her body, and her heart skittered out of control. Would he turn around? Put his arms around her? She didn't know if she wanted him to or not.

"I'd help out a lot more often if this is the kind of thanks I get," he said, smiling over his shoulder at her.

She chuckled and pulled free. "Are you flirting with me?"

"I can't. I'm not allowed."

"Well, maybe sometimes it's okay."

He shut off the water and turned around, folding his arms across his chest. "This is an interesting development."

"I said sometimes." She grabbed her bucket and headed for the bathroom, praying the fan had done its job.

It still smelled awful.

Easton muttered something and his footsteps left the house, returning several moments later. A few minutes after that "Mysterious Ways" by U2 floated into the room. Lani smiled, allowing the beat to bolster her mood even more. When she heard Easton's voice join in with Bono's, she pushed up from the tub she'd been scouring and peeked out the door. Easton moved to the rhythm of the music as he danced around the kitchen island, wiping down the counter.

When he saw her watching, he didn't stop like she expected. His movements became more exaggerated and ridiculous, and he raised his voice to say, "I can't hear you singing, Lani."

The song had just arrived at the chorus, so she lifted her chin and belted out the first line.

He grinned, pointing a finger at her, and picked up the words where she'd left off. "She's all right, she's all right, she's all right. Lani moves in mysterious ways!"

She laughed and returned to the bathroom, her voice still joining in on the fun. With music and Easton, the work sped by, and two hours later, while an Eagles song played, Ahe showed up with Taavatti. Lani had just finished vacuuming, and Easton was cleaning the last of the windows. If Taavatti could work some magic with the stains on the carpet, all Lani had left was to make the beds and stock the shelves and drawers with clean towels.

Feeling happier than she'd been all day, Lani gave Taavatti a big hug. "Mahalo for coming. I owe you big-time for this."

"No need," he said. "You 'ohana."

"Where's my mahalo?" Ahe opened his arms wide, and Lani walked into them, hugging him as well.

"Mahalo, Ahe," she said. "I'll repay you both with a year's supply of banana bread. How does that sound?"

Ahe slapped a kiss on her forehead while Taavatti grinned, saying, "Now that, I will take."

"What about you, Easton?" Lani said, extracting herself from Ahe's embrace. "Are you a fan of banana bread?"

"I am," he said, giving her a sly look. "But if I have a choice, I prefer the kind of thanks you gave me earlier."

Whether he'd said that to get a blush from Lani or a reaction from Ahe, both worked. Lani felt her cheeks warm while Ahe glared. Then he stalked over to Easton and picked up the spray bottle. "I can take it from here."

Easton handed over his rag. "Considering it's all done, of course you can." Then he grabbed his phone and unplugged the speakers, silencing the Eagles. The feeling in the room went from being lively to heavy in an instant.

"See you later," Easton said to Lani as he walked out the door.

She watched him go before snatching the rag from Ahe. "Why do you have to be such a *huki 'ino* sometimes? You're the one who asked for his help."

"I don't like how he looks at you."

"Get over it, Ahe."

"Lani." The way he said her name made it sound like he was censuring her and apologizing at the same time.

"Don't *Lani* me. He's my friend, just like you. And he deserves to be treated with respect, just like you."

His eyes narrowed. "You have to earn respect to deserve it. He hasn't earned mine yet."

"And what will it take to do that?"

His jaw clenched, and his mouth remained closed.

Lani nodded. "Exactly." Then she handed him the rag, pointed to the largest window in the room, and said, "You said you could take it from here, so enjoy yourself with that one."

Taavatti chose that moment to turn on the cleaner, and the loud noise of the motor kept Ahe from answering. While he cleaned the window, Lani changed the sheets and restocked shelves, and Taavatti got out the worst of the stains. By the time the Stradlings showed up at two, the Hema room was ready for them.

That night, when Mrs. Platt called to cancel her reservation for the Akua room, Lani put down the phone without wondering about the strangeness of it all. Pearl had been a gem of a guest—gracious, tidy, and wonderful company for Puna. If the Blacks didn't call next week to cancel their reservation, Lani was ready to do it for them.

chapter 13

L ani glanced through the darkness up the hill at the bungalow. It was nearing eleven o'clock, but the lights were still on. Was Easton still awake? She hadn't meant to spend so much time at Ahe's, but it couldn't be helped. Earlier, she'd made a dozen loaves of banana bread as thanks. She'd delivered six to Taavatti and meant to drop off four at Ahe's, but his mother had invited her in and it had taken over two hours to make it out. Ahe had welcomed her with a hug, showing her that any hard feelings between them were in the past as she knew they would be. When it came to family, Ahe never stayed upset for long.

By the time Lani made it home, her back ached, her head throbbed, and she longed for her bed. But she'd saved a loaf of banana bread for Easton and didn't know if she should deliver it tonight or in the morning. Her body cried out for morning, but other guests might be around and make it awkward, so Lani drew in a deep breath and headed up the hill. Through the open windows, Easton sat on the couch, typing away on his laptop.

Her heart skipped at the sight of him. His red Nike t-shirt was rumpled and his hair mussed, as though he'd raked his fingers through it more than once.

Lani was about to jog up the steps when quiet music began playing. She recognized the chorus of "Sweet Caroline" by Neil Diamond before Easton glanced at his watch with a frown and quickly answered his phone.

"Caro? What's wrong?" Then he laughed. "Sadie, honey, does your mama know you're awake and have her phone?"

He laughed again and rested his head against the back of the couch. "You little thief. Shouldn't you be asleep right now? It's five o'clock in the morning there." A pause. "Why can't you sleep? . . . Oh, I see. So what's it going to take to get you back in bed? . . . A story?" He chuckled. "You drive a hard bargain, little Sades, but tell you what. If you go crawl in bed right now and take the phone with you, I'll tell you the story about Lady Sadie and her slippery spider. Do we have a deal? . . . Awesome. Tell me when you're in bed."

He paused, his lips lifted, his eyes shining with humor. A moment later, he said, "Promise? . . . Okay, a deal's a deal. Once upon a time in a dark and dreary forest, there lived a very hairy, very large, and very blue spider named Goliath . . ."

Lani sank down on the bottom step and listened to a tale about a scary-looking spider and a beautiful little girl who wasn't afraid of him. Lani had always loved the timbre of Easton's voice, but listening to him now was magical. He pulled her into the charming story and held her captive until his voice began to lull her asleep.

She rested her head against the railing and her eyes drifted shut. It wasn't until she heard him say, "Sades, you still there?" that she started back awake.

"Goodnight, beautiful girl," Easton's voice floated

quietly through the window, and Lani wondered what it would feel like if those words had been meant for her. "I'll see you in six weeks and counting."

Her eyes opened all the way. Six weeks. Easton would be leaving in six weeks.

Why did that news rattle her like it had come out of nowhere? Summer was halfway over. Of course he was leaving in six weeks. He'd promised Sadie he would.

But it hurt to hear him spell it out so clearly, with no hesitation at all. Six weeks and he'd get to see Sadie again. He probably couldn't wait.

Lani pulled herself up, crept up the last few stairs, and left the plastic-wrapped loaf on the small bistro table before hurrying away. She'd been a fool to think that a friendship with him would keep her heart safe.

"Good evening, Lani," Pearl's mellow voice intruded on her troubled thoughts.

Lani spied Pearl on her lanai, sipping what looked like tea. Pearl always preferred hot chocolate in the mornings and tea at night.

Lani forced a smile to her lips. "You're up late tonight."

"I'm always up late." Pearl lifted her face to the sky. "Especially on clear nights like this when I can see so many stars. Aren't they lovely?"

Lani glanced up, noticing them for the first time tonight. Like a mass of little white Christmas lights, they glittered across the inky black sky in a promise of hope.

"They look so far away—so . . . untouchable." *Like Easton*, Lani thought.

"Yes, but their light still manages to touch us every night," said Pearl in her thoughtful way. "I guess they're sort of like people, in that respect. You don't have to physically touch someone to touch their heart."

Pearl continued to gaze at the stars as though she could see more than what the average person saw. She had an inner peace that radiated from her like soft starlight, making Lani wonder how many hearts Pearl had touched over the years.

"You and Easton seem to be getting along well," said Pearl suddenly, her eyes now trained on Lani.

Not wanting to talk about him, Lani shrugged. "We've become friends."

"Friends is always a good place to start."

"A good place to stay, too."

"Sometimes yes and sometimes no. It depends."

"This time, it's no," said Lani. "In six weeks, he'll fly away, and I'll never see him again. Just like I'll likely never see you after you leave." She paused, remembering the first real conversation she'd had with Pearl in this very spot. "You told me once that it must be hard to see so many people come and go. I think I understand what you meant now." Weariness took its unforgiving hold, and Lani mustered a small smile. "I'm off to bed. Good night, Pearl."

"Good night, Lani," she answered.

Easton squinted into the morning light and almost walked past the loaf of bread before he spotted it. Covered in plastic wrap, it glistened with dew. Right away, he knew who had made it and where it had come from, so he picked it up, took it inside, and quickly cut himself a slice, which he savored all the way down to the lanai at the main house.

Pearl was sitting alone at one of the tables, reading a book and sipping hot chocolate.

"What are you reading?" Easton asked, taking a seat next to her.

She closed the book, revealing a picture of a large, lily-like flower on the cover with the title, *Mystical Plants and Their Uses*. "It's a book about unique and rare plants. You'd probably find it a little dry."

"I'll admit, I don't have a lot of interest in horticulture, but I'm a fan of rare and unique."

She studied him for a moment, her expression curious. "Are you?"

"Most definitely."

"Love is rare and unique. Are you a fan of that?"

Caught off guard and made suddenly uncomfortable by the directness of her question, Easton sat back in his chair and chuckled. "To be honest, I'm not sure how to answer that. I'm not even sure how we got here. Weren't we talking about plants?"

Pearl folded her hands over the book and leaned forward, searching his eyes for what, Easton wasn't sure. "There's a remarkable night-blooming cactus called Queen of the Night. It's rarely found in the wild and looks a lot like Medusa's hair, if you can imagine that, with snake-like branches weaving out from the root stem. If you were to stumble across it, you'd think it unremarkable and even ugly. But one night every summer, it produces the most exquisite white and fragrant flowers that stay in bloom only for that one night. By the time the sun awakens, the bloom closes tight, never to open again."

And just like that, they were back to plants. Good. Even better, what she'd said had piqued his interest. "Where do they grow?"

"In tropical locations."

"Like Maui?"

"More like Indonesia."

"Oh." For a second, Easton had been sure she'd tell him

where he might find the plant nearby, but apparently that's not why she'd brought it up.

"Love is like the Queen of the Night's flower, you know. It doesn't bloom often, but when it does it's exquisite. The trick is noticing before it closes up and withers away."

Ah, back to love again. Easton had to laugh. From the day he'd first met Pearl, she had intrigued him with her metaphors, wisdom, and grace. She had an almost mystical aura about her that seemed to defy time and space. Or maybe Easton wanted to believe that because he wanted to believe that Fate was somehow working its mysterious hand to bring him and Lani together.

But that was crazy.

"You sound like you speak from experience," he finally said.

"Oh, I do. Lots of experience."

"Did you notice when love came your way?"

Her eyes widened as though the question had taken her aback. But her surprise gave way to melancholy. "I noticed. It was he who did not—at least not until our chance had withered away."

Easton was immediately sorry he'd asked. Before now, Pearl had always seemed incapable of feeling sadness or any of the other less desirable human emotions.

"I'm so sorry," he said.

She waved off his apology, and her bright, serene smile returned. "It was a difficult time for me, but looking back, I wouldn't change a thing. Every experience—good and bad— has the power to mold and change us into something greater than we were before."

"Or worse than we were before."

She tapped his knee with her petite finger. "Only if you let the experience break you. Otherwise, it's always for the better. Sometimes you see it right away and other times it takes moving forward and looking back. How else are traits like empathy, compassion, and understanding developed if not through struggle and pain?"

A light breeze blew a few leaves onto their table, and Easton swept them away with his hand. "I have to say, Pearl, that every conversation I have with you leaves me with a lot to think about."

She smiled and patted his knee. "Thinking is always good, but sometimes action is better."

The door opened, and Lani breezed out wearing a peach floral shirt and white capris. With her hair in a loose diagonal braid, she looked like a breath of fresh air and probably smelled like it too. Easton's eyes stayed on her as she set the juice on the counter, along with a bowl of ice and individually-packaged yogurts.

Then he pushed his chair back and approached her. "That banana bread was the best I've ever had. If I was the baking sort, I would get your recipe."

Her mouth lifted into a smile. "You don't bake?"

"Not if I can help it. But I like baked things and frequent bakeries as often as possible."

She laughed softly, and the sound floated around him like a gentle breeze. Lately, he couldn't be around her and not feel lighter.

"Have any fun plans today?" she said.

"I was going to ask you the same thing."

She made a face. "Not unless you think driving the Hāna Highway is fun. I ordered something online last month, and I need to go pick it up at a store in Haiku."

"Want some company?" Easton blurted before even thinking about it. Did he really want to spend half the day on the world's windiest road when he had his own work to do?

Yes, came the thought. If Lani was along for the ride, that would be a definite yes.

Why wasn't she saying anything? Why did she look like she was trying to come up with a polite way to say, *Thanks, but no thanks*? She really didn't want to make such a tedious drive alone, did she? Or was being alone preferable to being with him?

"Thanks. I really appreciate the offer, but after all your help yesterday, I could never let you do that."

"What are you talking about?" he teased. "You've already repaid me."

Her expression turned rueful. "One loaf of banana bread is nothing."

Easton leaned in close. "I wasn't talking about the bread."

A faint blush appeared on her cheeks, and she flicked a quick glance at Pearl before clearing her throat. "Really, thanks for the offer, but I'm good. I'm sure you have other things you need to do, like writing? How's your book coming anyway?" She phrased the question like a challenge, as though daring him to tell her more.

Now it was Easton's turn to feel uncomfortable. He'd rather talk about the latest chick flick or rare and unique flowers than his writing. What was going on? It felt like something had changed between yesterday and today, and he had no idea what.

The only thing he did know was that she didn't want him coming with her. "You're right. I do have some things I need to get done today."

She nodded. "The forecast predicts rain this afternoon, so you might be doing some of your writing indoors."

"I'll keep that in mind."

She drew in a breath and looked at Pearl. "Aloha, Pearl. How are you this morning?"

"Lovely."

"Puna will be out in a second. She's waiting for some muffins to finish baking. I hear she challenged you to another game of Mahjong?"

Pearl laughed. "Yes. She's become quite addicted to the game, I'm afraid."

"Yet another reason I'm glad you're still with us. I hope you have a beautiful day."

Lani glanced at Easton, gave him a quick head nod, then did a double-take. Her eyes widened, focusing on his shoulder. "I don't believe it," she whispered.

Easton looked down and saw something move on his shirt. He lifted his hand to swat it away, but Lani grabbed it before he could. "Don't." She moved close enough that he could smell her apple and flowery shampoo. "Do you know what that is?"

"A hairy moth?" he guessed, craning his head to see it.

"It's a Hawaiian Blue butterfly," she said reverently. The wings opened, revealing an almost turquoise center that fanned to a dark gray. The wings were much prettier open.

"I thought I saw one of these a few weeks ago," she said, "but I didn't get a good enough look to be sure. I read about them when I first moved here, and I've wanted to see one ever since. And now here it is. Isn't it beautiful?"

Easton had seen more beautiful butterflies—the American Lady in Colombia, the Blue Morpho in Mexico, and the Golden Cocoon in Malaysia. But he knew the thrill of a long-awaited reward, so he could understand her excitement. But would he really be forced to stand here all day while she admired an insect instead of him?

And the morning had dawned with such promise.

The butterfly must have sensed his ill-will because it fluttered its textured wings and took flight. Lani followed it for a few steps, resting her hands on the railing of the lanai as it flew into the sun and was swallowed up in the morning light.

She spun around. "Did you see that, Pearl?"

Pearl nodded. "In China, the butterfly is a symbol of love."

Easton had to cough to cover up his laughter. He wondered if Pearl would tell Lani about the cactus love-flower.

"Really?" Lani asked, her voice a bit too high-pitched to be genuine. "That's interesting." Then she sidled past Easton and headed for the house. "I should see if Puna needs some help."

Easton watched her go, wondering about rare butterflies and cactus flowers and afternoon rain. But mostly he wondered what had gone wrong since yesterday.

"Pearl," he said slowly. "I'm not sure I'll ever understand women."

"How dull life would be if you did."

chapter 14

A quick rap on the front door was the only warning Ahe gave before he burst inside the house and trotted into the great room. Lani wasn't surprised because it was a normal thing for him to do. As soon as he'd considered them family, he had made himself right at home.

Lani clicked mute on the show she and Puna were watching and eyed him expectantly.

"It hasn't rained for two days, and it's a full moon tonight." Ahe was a little out of breath, and his dark eyes glittered with excitement.

A full moon and no rain could only mean one thing. Ahe wanted to go to Kapu Aina. Lani glanced at the TV, where a documentary on rainforests continued in silence. It was the only thing on TV that was remotely interesting.

"You really have to think about this one?" Puna held her hand out for the remote, turned off the TV then waved dismissively at her granddaughter. "Go. Live," she said.

Lani laughed, but didn't need any more coaxing than

that. She'd developed a great love for Kapu Aina the first time Ahe had invited her along. During the day, it was beautiful and peaceful—the perfect escape—but under the light of the full moon, it became magical.

"I'll meet you out front," she told Ahe on her way to her room.

Lani quickly changed into a swimsuit, quick-dry shorts, and a tank, then found Ahe in the hallway, waiting impatiently. He grabbed her arm and pulled her outside, where a group of people were already piled in the back of his pickup. From the corner of her eye, Lani caught sight of Easton walking down from the bungalow, wearing board shorts, a t-shirt, and Tevas.

She felt a twinge of anxiety. Was he planning to finagle an invite? No. She wouldn't let him. Not to Kapu Aina. For once, she was grateful for Ahe's animosity toward Easton. He would make sure—

"I invited the haole," said Ahe in her ear, slinging his arm around her back to give her a side hug. "See? Even I can be nice sometimes."

Wait. Ahe had already invited him? Lani could have kicked herself for ever going to bat for Easton. Ahe was probably expecting a mahalo, a hug, or at the very least, a smile, but Lani couldn't do any of those things. If Easton came with them, his memory would be imprinted on one of her favorite spots on the island, and she'd never be able to escape there without thinking of him. It was selfish, but Lani wanted Kapu Aina to stay hers and Ahe's and the rest of her local friends.

Of all the ways Ahe could have extended an olive branch, why Kapu Aina?

Someone called out to Ahe, saving Lani from answering, and she crawled into the back of the pickup with everyone else. People scooted aside, leaving just enough room for her and Easton to sit hip-to-hip and shoulder-to-shoulder. She tensed, wanting to crawl right back out and make up some excuse why she couldn't go anymore. But Ahe would never hear of it—not now that she'd already agreed.

Lani shouldn't have come. She should have continued watching the documentary with Puna and let the moonlight swim happen without her.

"You look happy to see me," Easton said, just loud enough for her to hear.

Lani ignored the comment and tried to do the same to him. But they were sitting too close, and her body was too aware.

Maybe she could talk him out of coming.

"This hike isn't for the faint-hearted," she said. "You sure you want to come?"

"I'll do my best not to faint."

Just like he'd do his best not to take a hint. "How do you feel about cliff jumping?" she tried again, hoping he had a paralyzing fear of heights.

"Love it." He craned his head to the side to get a better look at her. "I take it you're a fan as well?"

She refused to look at him. "You sound surprised."

"Maybe I am," he said. "Though after watching the way you surf, I probably shouldn't be. You seem to be very at-one with the water."

She couldn't resist a quick peek in his direction. He wore no hat, and his hair glistened as though he'd just gotten out of the shower. As Ahe's truck bumped its way onto Hāna Highway, Lani's shoulder rammed into Easton's. Her hopes plummeted. They were officially off, and Lani's fate was sealed. Easton would be coming with them whether she wanted him to or not.

All around them others laughed and joked and enjoyed. Lani mourned.

"What does Kapu Aina mean?" Easton asked, pulling her from self-pitying thoughts.

"Forbidden land."

"Is it on privately owned land or something?"

"No. It's just. . . untouched." She adjusted to a more comfortable position and leaned her head back. "Ahe's grandfather loved to explore the island. He came to know it so well that he could go off for days without food or water or the fear of getting lost—at least that's how Ahe tells it. His family tends to embellish all stories, so I never know what to believe, but it sounds cool."

"I take it Ahe's grandfather discovered Kapu Aina? Did I say that right?"

"Yes and yes."

"And they've kept it a secret ever since?"

"They share it with friends and family, and even a few outsiders like me."

He nudged her shoulder with his. "What are you talking about? You're Ahe's *sistah*."

She swallowed and nodded, knowing Hāna wouldn't be Hāna without this group of friends. "They're good people."

Easton pulled his knees closer to his chest and glanced up at the sky. "Is there a reason we're going so late? We won't have light for much longer."

"We'll have enough to hike there—or, at least mostly there, and the full moon will give us enough to find our way back. And when the light hits the water just right, you'll understand."

"Can't wait."

Twenty minutes later, Ahe turned onto a bumpy, windy, dirt road and didn't slow his speed at all. They jerked, they bounced, they weaved, and Easton leaned forward with a groan, putting his head between his knees. "You didn't warn me about this part," he muttered.

"You get motion sickness?" she asked.

"Only when riding backwards on windy, bumpy roads."

She laughed. "I'm surprised. Though after watching the way *you* surf, I probably shouldn't be."

"I'm glad you find my pain and amateur surfing skills so entertaining," came his muffled response. "We almost there?"

"Not even close."

He groaned, she laughed, and Ahe slammed on the breaks, skidding to a stop. Several people cursed Ahe's name, including Easton, and everyone began leaping out of the truck.

Easton lifted his head, revealing a pale, almost green face. "I thought we weren't close."

"We're not," said Lani, swinging her legs over the side. "We still have about four miles to hike." She hopped down and turned around, offering him a smile. "Coming?"

He didn't need to be told twice. In a fluid movement, he jumped over the side and landed next to her, pointing his finger at her. "You're evil."

"And you're gullible."

He rolled his eyes and looked around. "Where are we?"

"About to enter the forbidden lands, remember?" She began following the fifteen others who were already on their way up the mountain. Easton trailed behind.

"Ho, Lani!" Ahe called. "Where are you?"

"Coming." She quickened her steps to catch up to him, grateful for an excuse to put some distance between her and Easton. Maybe if she stuck with Ahe the rest of the night, Easton's imprint wouldn't be as deep.

Ahe slapped Pika's bare chest with the back of his hand then said to Lani. "Tell this *lolo* that we saw a wild boar right here this same time last year."

"He's lying," said Lani without hesitation.

Ahe's eyes bulged and he laughed. "You *fo real,* Lani? You saw it too! Where's Paavo? He'll tell you."

Ahe was right. Lani *had* seen the boar. But she also happened to know that Pika's grandmother had been bitten by a wild boar and later died from some infection because of it. Or, at least that was the story going around. Regardless, she didn't want to say anything that might make Pika break into a sweat. He was still young and trying his hardest to prove his manliness.

But Ahe wouldn't care about any of that, so Lani was quick to redirect the conversation. "What I remember is seeing you trip over a root then lose your shoe in a mud pit."

Ahe stopped looking for his friend as she knew he would. Despite his large, muscular body, he was as easily distracted as a child. He threw back his head and laughed at the memory. "Now you see why we wait for a full moon *and* no rain. I need my shoes."

Lani laughed. "You need your shoes for standing around? I thought we were planning to hike tonight."

"Patience, Lani. Patience." But he turned anyway, and the group surged forward. As they hiked, they stepped over large roots and ducked under low branches, careful to not leave too much of a trail. Ahe continued down memory lane like always, recounting story after story about Kapu Aina. Lani couldn't remember having a conversation with Ahe about ideas or thoughts or even goals for the future. He preferred to live in the moment and relive past moments. And so she listened while he talked, making a comment here or a correction there to show she was paying attention.

Every so often, Lani would glance back, but too many people blocked her view of Easton. His laugh and voice occasionally caught up to her, so she knew he'd found someone to chat with. It impressed her how easily he could fit in anywhere. A dry comment here, a question there, and everyone, with the exception of Ahe, seemed to like him. She wondered who had made him laugh and tried not to be bothered that it wasn't her.

After about thirty minutes, they met up with the river and the first and smallest of three waterfall jumps. It could easily be skirted by climbing down a dense tree on the opposite side, but no one climbed down. Anyone who couldn't take this jump should turn back now. They only got taller from here.

A break in the canopy of trees overhead allowed the fading sunlight to highlight the water to the left of the deepest spot in the pool below. Ahe jumped first, followed by Pika and some of the others. Lani purposefully stayed back, allowing those between her and Easton to go ahead.

"How tall is this one?" Easton asked when he caught up.

Lani shrugged. "Tall enough to know you're falling before you hit."

They were standing to the left of the river, and he took a step forward, peeking over the edge. "My guess is thirty feet," he said, gesturing for her to go ahead. "Ladies first? So I can see the safe place to land."

Lani made sure the path was clear before she jumped. She felt a moment's rush of adrenalin before her body landed in the frigid waters. That first dip always zinged her, but it was a warm evening, and her body would soon adjust. She swam out of the way and turned around in time to see Easton tuck his knees to his chest before he hit the water. His splash re-soaked several people, making them curse Easton's name, and Ahe, already out of the river, laughed.

"You alright sometimes, haole," shouted Ahe. "Good for a laugh anyway."

"Glad I'm good for something," he muttered to Lani as he swam past to the side of the river. Once he'd lifted his body out, he extended a hand to her.

She hesitated only a moment before accepting his help. He easily pulled her out of the water and grinned. "Haven't fainted yet."

"That jump was nothing compared to the others," said Lani, pulling her hand free. But instead of catching up to Ahe like she should do, she stayed with Easton. She needed a break from all the "remember whens" and knew that Easton would either leave her to her thoughts or start an actual discussion.

But as they walked, it was Lani who started it. "The other night I heard you talking to . . . Sadie, is it?" At his lifted eyebrow, she rushed on to add, "I didn't mean to eavesdrop. I was planning to hand-deliver the bread. But your window was open and your phone rang and . . . I eavesdropped."

He chuckled and held a large and leafy branch out of her way. "Little Sade—she has me wrapped around her adorable, five-year-old finger. Apparently her mom, my sister Caroline, taught her how to call me. So when she woke up in the middle of the night, she snuck Caro's phone and put her new skills to the test. I've been getting about a call a day ever since. I haven't told my sister yet because I don't want them to stop."

Lani smiled a little. What would it be like to have a niece or nephew who knew and liked her well enough to want to call every day? Lani wouldn't know. She had one of each but had only seen pictures of them on Facebook or Instagram. One lived in Ohio, the other in Tennessee. They probably didn't even know her name.

"You said you'd see her soon. I take it that means you're headed home after this trip?"

He nodded. "I go home after all my trips. At least for a few weeks. It's how I recuperate."

The conversation was drilling little holes in Lani's heart. He sounded so unaffected, as though the thought of leaving didn't bother him at all. She wasn't sure why she'd brought it up. Perhaps because a small part of her—the one that still believed in fairy tales and happily ever afters—hoped that he *wouldn't* sound unaffected. That maybe, just maybe, his feelings had sunk to the bottom of the deep end like hers.

"Your book will be finished by then?" she asked.

Easton moved another branch out of her way, and she ducked under his arm. When he didn't say anything, she wondered if he'd ignored the question completely or was thinking of a way to change the subject like he always did.

When he finally spoke, he surprised her. "I'm not writing a book, Lani."

It was honest—more honest than he'd ever been about the career aspect of his life. It felt big, like he was about to trust her with something he didn't trust with just anyone. Her heart thumped, and Lani turned around, slowing her steps.

"What are you writing?"

"Articles."

"For what?"

He shrugged, looking off to the side. "Magazines. My blog."

"What sort of articles?"

"Basically, they're short stories about my experiences around the world."

Walking slowly backwards, Lani's foot caught on a root. She started to fall, but Easton grabbed her hand, keeping her upright. When she regained her footing, she stood only a few breaths away.

He was so close. She could see the light scruff on his face, the flecks of dark brown in his eyes. But the closeness she felt with him now had nothing to do with proximity. "Why did it take you this long to tell me that? I think it's cool. I had no idea magazines paid so well for articles."

He looked away and let go of her arm. "We're falling behind."

And just like that the connection severed. Lani's hope extinguished like a tiki torch with no oil. He'd given her a glimpse, but no more. She turned around and continued walking, not ready to give up. "Are you a trust fund kid or something?"

He laughed. "If I were, do you think I'd be sleeping on a hard bed in a gecko-infested shack rather than staying at the Travaasa?"

"Are there a lot of geckos in your room?"

"Yes," he said, chuckling again.

"I'm so sorry. I will—"

"Do what? Call the exterminator and kill the peaceful wall-climbers? Don't you dare. They're fun to watch and honestly don't bother me."

There he was again, the easy Easton. The kind Easton. The Easton that had found his way into Lani's heart and would rip it to shreds in just over five weeks. Like a bad omen, Lani could see it coming and felt powerless to stop it. Every word, every touch, every glance, and she fell a little bit farther. Her grandmother always spoke of soaring, she just never mentioned the crash landing that could easily follow.

"Ever tried to catch one?" she asked. "They're pretty quick."

"Nope. Haven't really had the desire. But you never know when a moment of insanity might strike, so I won't say I never will."

"I caught one once," said Lani. "A few years ago, some guests brought their little girl to stay. She was a toddler—probably about three or four—and loved to drag her mom outside to find the "yizzuds," as she called them. After the first day, I could tell her mom was growing tired of the gecko hunts, so I took over a few times. The second time, we found one lounging in the sun, and I was able to grab it before it could get away. We put it in an old fish aquarium with some plants and leaves and fed it live crickets." Lani smiled at the memory. "Bella never cared about hunting for them again after that, and I made a new best friend."

"And the parents loved you for it."

Her smile turned rueful. "At least until Bella declared she wanted to take her 'yizzud' home with her. When her parents said no, that didn't go over very well."

Easton chuckled. "I imagine there was a lot of weeping and wailing."

"It was pretty sad," Lani said. "I had to tell her that the lizard's mommy and daddy wanted their baby back and promise that we'd catch another one the next time she came."

"Have they ever come back?"

"No. At least not to our place."

"Do you have any regular guests?" he asked.

"A few. They've fallen in love with Hāna and try to return about once a year. Those are the ones who become good friends, and we stay in touch with most of them." As they passed a shrub, Lani pulled off a leaf and rolled it into a tight cylinder. Would Easton become a reoccurring guest? No. He wrote about his experiences traveling, so of course he couldn't repeat his trips. The very nature of his career made him a been-there-done-that-off-to-something-new kind of traveler.

Lani tossed the leaf aside. Why did she keep doing this to herself? She'd been taught by Ahe to live for the moment, learn from the past, and not worry about the future. Live, breathe, wonder, and love—it was that simple—and she'd embraced it wholeheartedly until Derek's proposal and Easton's arrival. Now she couldn't stop worrying about the present and future state of her heart, and how she'd recover once Easton flew away.

"I have a question for you," said Easton from behind.

A twig snapped from somewhere up ahead and murmuring voices could be heard. They were catching up to the rest of the group.

"Is it one I have to answer?" she asked. "If so, then it's only fair that I get to do the same."

"It's a question you probably won't be able to answer," he said.

"What?" She stopped and glanced back at him. "Why ask a question if I won't have an answer?"

"Because it's a game, and it's fun."

"For whom? You?"

He grinned. "Yes. Now listen. Cowboy Bill rode into town on Friday. Three days later he rode out of town on Friday. Can you explain that?"

"A riddle? Really?"

"Bet you can't figure it out."

"And if I do?"

"Then you're smarter than I am. One of my nephews asked me the same thing the last time I was home, and it took me a solid thirty minutes of questioning before I figured it out."

Lani turned around and began walking again. "Then I'll wait thirty-five minutes to answer so you won't feel bad. How's that?"

"Do you know the answer?"

She pulled another leaf off a bush and twirled it between her fingers. "Of course."

"Then tell me."

"I will. In thirty-five minutes."

He laughed. "Don't pretend to be all philanthropic. Admit it. You're stalling because you have no idea."

"Maybe I am and maybe I'm not. Guess you'll never know." The group was standing near the next waterfall, waiting for a turn to jump. Lani's clothes were still damp from the previous dip, but even though the sun had begun to dim, she wasn't cold.

One after another, they all leapt from the second fall, waiting only long enough for the person in front of them to get out of the way. Easton glanced down, guessed the height to be about fifty feet, then asked Lani if she wanted to jump first.

"You go first this time," she said.

"Okay." Without a hint of hesitation, he leapt off the top of the fall, spinning a 180 as he dropped. As he hit the water below with his hands flat against his chest, Lani's stomach gave a little lurch. Even though she'd made this jump dozens of times, that first step off still didn't come as easy as Easton had made it look. And this was nothing to what awaited them next.

The moment the pool below was clear, Lani took a deep breath and leapt. Air whizzed past her, blaring in her ears like a high-powered fan, and the spray from the falls slapped her arms before she hit the water. This was why she loved to jump—this exact moment—when two elements came together.

She resurfaced, feeling chilled once again, but invigorated and ready for the next jump.

Again, Easton had waited to extend her a hand. As soon as she was out, he said, "Any thoughts on Cowboy Bill yet?"

Lani rinsed the worst of the dirt from her Chaco sandals and squeezed the excess water from her ponytail and tank. Then she glanced at her watch. "I'll have a comment in fourteen minutes. No wait. Make that thirteen."

"I think you're more stubborn than me."

"Wouldn't that be something?" She smiled, then looked up to find Ahe watching them from a few yards ahead. Without saying anything, he turned around and began hiking, his movements a little less relaxed than usual.

Lani sighed. She knew Ahe had some feelings for her. How deep they ran, she wasn't sure, but they did run. He'd made it obvious over the years in his light-hearted, sometimes-possessive way. But he also knew that she thought of him as a brother and nothing more—at least she hoped he did. She'd done her best to make that clear. If only he'd fall for one of the local girls who had been mooning over him, then everything would be good.

"Why does Ahe think of me as a threat?" asked Easton, who'd apparently followed her gaze and was now watching her closely.

"I don't know," said Lani. "I guess he thinks it's possible for me to get swept off my feet in a matter of weeks and feels the need to keep it from happening."

"Is it possible?" Easton asked, his Adam's apple bobbing. Although his lips were half lifted in a teasing smile, his eyes showed a hint of seriousness.

"Please," was all she said, even though she was being swept off and then some. But she wasn't about to tell him that—not when he'd made it clear that he still stood firmly on solid ground. Nor would she let him read it in her expression either.

"The horse's name was Friday," she blurted. Then she pushed past him to catch up to everyone else.

chapter 15

Piko had fallen to the back of the pack and sauntered next to a sweet girl named Kaia. Lani quickened her steps to chat with them for a few minutes before catching up to the next small group. She was nearly to Ahe when they reached The Crack.

A crevice between two large boulders, The Crack made Ahe suck in all the way to squeeze his way though. It was slow-going, inch by inch, but eventually they all wiggled their way out. After that, Lani found a pebble and kicked it, Ahe followed suit, and Paavo joined in as well. It became a game of who could kick the rock the farthest, and it lasted until they reach the final jump.

At the base of the sixty-five-foot falls was Kapu Aina. Darkness had fallen, but the moon highlighted the ripples in the water below. It beckoned Lani, luring her to pools with the promise of peace, warmth, and serenity.

She jumped first. As the air and falls whooshed past her, she felt like she was falling through a porthole into a fantasy world where colors were more vibrant, plants more fragrant, and the water softer. She landed in a cool gush of bubbles and resurfaced with a grin, immediately making her way to the other side.

One of the things that made Kapu Aina so great was the hot thermal springs that fed one side of the pool. Lani found her favorite spot near one of the springs and let the heat warm her body. She laid her head back and closed her eyes, feeling the moonlight wash over her as she listened to the roar of the falls, people jumping, talking, laughing, the yelps, the splashes, the faint sounds of leaves rustling from behind. How lucky was she to be able to live this life every day?

"You didn't wait the full thirty-five minutes," said Easton. "Nor did you bother warning me about that last jump. I think that's the highest waterfall I've ever thrown myself off. I'll admit, it wigged me out a bit."

"But you still did it." Lani kept her eyes closed, not ready to be pulled away from her happy place of peace.

"Only because I didn't want to lose face and knew I'd never find my way back on my own. And wow, the water is warm over here. Are you trying to hoard it all to yourself?"

"Everyone will come once they've had their fun," she murmured. "In the meantime, shush."

He did, and Lani smiled. Everyone else was making a ruckus, but at least Easton had taken the—

"Mind if I ask you another question?"

"Yes," she said.

Water sloshed, his arm bumped against hers, and she could feel him settle in beside her. His voice dropped to an almost-whisper. "Just tell me this: How are we supposed to get back to the truck?"

Despite the warmth of the water, goosebumps broke out all over her body. She opened one eye and squinted at him.

His gaze was on the top of the large waterfall, his eyebrow lifted in a *Please don't tell me we're going to have to climb that to get out* expression.

Lani's smile widened.

"You're only now wondering that?"

"I'm only now voicing that," he said. "Tell me there's a hidden elevator inside that cliff somewhere."

"Yep. It'll take us to a secret bat cave where we'll have our pick of really cool ride-on toys."

"Sweet."

She laughed, then swiped her palm across the water and splashed him with a small wave, mostly to give her an excuse to scoot a little away from him. He splashed her back—in the face. She reciprocated with both hands, and he did the same—over and over again until she was laughing so hard, she could barely call out for reinforcements.

"Ahe!" she screamed between mouthfuls of water. "Come teach this haole a lesson!"

Ahe, Paavo, and Rab responded to her call for help. Easton stopped splashing long enough to realize three large Polynesians were closing in on him. He immediately lifted his hands in surrender. "We were just having a little fun, guys."

"Fun or no, Lani said to teach you a lesson, and we like to teach lessons," Ahe said as his two friends laughed.

Easton eyed them warily. "Lesson learned. We're good now. Right, Lani?"

Lani knew exactly what her friends would do to Easton if she let them. They'd give him a good dunking then toss him off one of the ledges near the side of the falls.

"I don't know," she said noncommittally. "You did get me pretty soaked."

"You were already soaked."

The gleam in Ahe's eyes made him look like a tiger ready to pounce, and Lani realized that he might take the retaliation a bit further than he normally would with anyone else. So Lani pointed above Easton's head and said, "What about a diving contest instead? From that middle ledge over there." She raised her voice to be heard by the others. "Kaia, Maaike, and I will be the judges. Yeah?"

The two other girls responded with cheers and clapping. Ahe agreed with, "Right on," and Easton shot Lani a look that said, *You'll pay for this later.*

She was sure he meant when Ahe wasn't around.

And so the contest began, with Easton being the first to scale the moss-covered boulders to the ledge. Once there, he took stock of his surroundings before leaping forward and executing an impressive one-and-a-half with a twist, finally diving into the water.

As soon as he surfaced, Ahe called from above, "*Ho tantaran*, take it easy."

Easton swam to Lani and said, "Do I want to know what that means?"

"Show off," she responded with a smile.

He smiled in return. "I think that's a step up from haole, don't you?"

She laughed, and Ahe jumped, one-upping Easton with a full double and a twist. He resurfaced and gave his mop of dark, curly hair a shake, grinning at Easton in triumph.

"Who's the *tantaran* now?" Easton said.

Ahe's grin widened—until Paavo flipped once and landed in a cannonball, giving Ahe a cold shower. The other guys jumped, then everyone jumped again. Eventually the girls wanted in on the fun so they joined in as well. No one noticed how late it was until the moon slipped behind the canopy of trees and a thicker darkness engulfed them.

Lani glanced at the sky with a frown, then sighed. "I hate to be the spoiler of fun, but I'd better head. I've got an early day tomorrow."

"Let your guests make their own *grind*," Ahe said, his legs dangling off the ledge above.

"Yeah, that would go over well at a bed and *breakfast*," she said.

"I should go too," added Maaike.

"Yeah, me too, *brah*," Rab said.

So they dragged themselves out of the pool and shoved their wet feet into damp sandals, saying goodbye to another beautiful night at Kapu Aina.

Easton caught Lani's arm before she could follow the others. He cleared his throat. "I just wanted to say thanks. Tonight was great."

"Ahe was the one who invited you," she reminded him.

"I have a feeling he wouldn't have if it wasn't for something you said."

Lani watched the last of the group disappear into the darkness. "I did say something, but I don't deserve any thanks for tonight. I probably wouldn't have invited you."

"Yeah," he said, his voice quiet. "I kind of got that vibe earlier." A pause. "Is there a reason you didn't want me here?"

When he was genuine like this, Lani felt her resistance melt. She sighed, trying to think of words that were honest and yet not too much.

"You're leaving in a few weeks, and . . . sometimes goodbyes are easier sooner than later, you know?"

He nodded, his expression solemn. "I'm not really one for goodbyes."

What did that mean? For a second, Lani felt a surge of hope that he was implying he didn't want to say goodbye—

not now or later—but the look on his face told her a different interpretation, and her hope vanished.

"I don't understand," she said.

He shrugged. "I hate saying goodbye, so I usually don't."

Lani still didn't understand. "How do you not say goodbye? You just pack your bags, leave a note on the counter, and slink away?"

"I don't leave notes either."

"I see," said Lani, though she really didn't.

"Goodbyes are uncomfortable and awkward, and I prefer to leave on a better note."

She gave his opinion some thought and found that she agreed with part of it—but only part. "Yes, they're uncomfortable, but they're also important. When you open a door that isn't meant to be kept open, you close it. Whether it's with a creak, a slam, or a quiet click, you close it."

Easton's eyes searched hers, shadowed and mysterious in the moonlight. He moved closer and clasped her hand, lifting it slowly, as though testing the waters, then threading his fingers through hers when she didn't pull away. "And what if I want to keep it open—at least a crack?"

A pounding echoed in Lani's ears, and her chest rose and fell as she struggled to keep her breath even. "I'm not much of a cracked-door person. If I open a door, I open it wide enough to let in the breeze, the sunshine, the smells, the sounds—everything."

He tugged her closer, and Lani caught a whiff of river water and nature. "So you're an all or nothing type of girl?"

She swallowed. "Anything less isn't worth it."

His other hand lifted her free hand, and he moved in even closer. Lani didn't know what was happening or if she wanted it to happen. He avoided goodbyes. She needed them. He liked cracks. She wanted all-the-way open. He moved around. She stayed put. All those things together made her feel like they were balancing on a paddleboard in the middle of a churning ocean and it was only a matter of time before they got thrown off—both in different directions.

He inched closer, and Lani's eyes drifted shut. Every ounce of self-preservation inside her screamed at her to run away, but the pull was too strong, and she couldn't. His breath warmed her mouth right before his lips brushed against hers in a feather-light touch. Her body trembled, feeling the push and pull between desire and good sense. How could something that felt so right not be right?

"Lani. Haole. You guys coming or wot?" Ahe's voice called from the blackness up ahead.

It was the splash of water Lani needed. She stepped back and pulled her hands free. "I'm sorry, but I can't do this."

He let out a breath and raked his fingers through his hair, making it spike on top. He looked like he wanted to argue or say something, but then he clenched his jaw and nodded. "We should go."

Instead of heading back the way they'd come, Lani followed the group to the south, where Rab had left his truck earlier, parked on his family's private property. As they walked, Lani couldn't help but wonder if Kapu Aina had just been made better—or worse.

The morning brought overcast skies, the threat of a shower, and no Lani. Everyone else had gathered for breakfast on the lanai, including Easton. Pearl sat with two new guests—two pretty sisters in their twenties who had tried more than once to strike up a flirtation with him. He'd sat at the next table over, alone, hoping Lani would come out and they could talk. But she didn't, and he'd finished his breakfast thirty minutes ago.

"Did you enjoy Kapu Aina last night?" Cora asked as she refilled his juice for the third time. Easton didn't want anymore, but continued to drink because it gave him an excuse to linger. If only he'd made it there before the sisters, then he could have been the one sharing a table—and interesting conversation—with Pearl.

"I did enjoy it, though it made for a late night. I take it Lani decided to sleep in?" He tried to sound casual, but from the twinkle in Cora's eyes, she didn't buy it.

"No. Lani never sleeps in. She was up before the sun and left a note saying she needed to run to Costco."

"Ah." Disappointment panged in his gut, but at least Easton knew it was pointless to stay. Which was just as well. For the first time since he'd stepped off the plane, he had definite plans for the day, and he wanted to get moving on them before the skies decided to let loose.

Before he could make his excuses, Cora took a seat next to him and leaned forward, resting her elbows on the table. Easton noticed that her curly, white hair was a bit frizzier than usual.

"Lani went to Costco a week and a half ago," she said in a pointed tone, as though she expected Easton to know why that was important information.

"That's . . . nice," he finally said.

Her mouth turned down, showing her annoyance that he hadn't picked up on whatever hint she was attempting to drop. "Before you came, she only made that trip once a month at the bare minimum. In the last seven weeks, she's gone four times."

Easton shifted positions, not seeing how he was responsible for that. If Lani felt the need to avoid him, she didn't have to drive all the way to Kahului. She could simply go to the beach or to downtown Hāna or even the Seven Sacred Pools. He wouldn't be anywhere near those places.

"Well," said Easton. "You are busier in the summer, right?"

"Not that much busier."

He let out a breath. "What do you want me to say, that I'm sorry? Because if I've done something to upset Lani—and I'm not sure what that would be—then I really am."

"I don't want your apology."

"Then what?"

She shook her head as though disappointed in him yet again. "You young people make things so much harder than they have to be. Isn't that right, Pearl?"

"Yes," Pearl answered immediately, apparently unashamed of the fact that she'd been eavesdropping.

"Why can't you admit your feelings and see what happens?" said Cora.

Easton shifted in his seat again, not sure if he should be having this conversation with Lani's grandmother while sitting within hearing distance of the other guests—though after this maybe the sisters would stop trying to flirt with him.

Regardless, Easton lowered his voice. "What if things go south?"

"What if they go north or east or west?" she countered. "You'll never know unless you try."

Everyone was watching him now. Normally, Easton didn't mind being the center of attention, but in this context, he'd rather not. He took one last sip of his juice and pushed his chair back. "Mahalo for a wonderful breakfast, Cora."

"You're very welcome," she said. "I hope you have a . . . directional day."

He had to chuckle at that. "I plan to."

chapter 16

Avoiding Easton came easy the last week of July, mostly because he wasn't around much. His car was gone when Lani got up in the morning and typically stayed gone until late in the day. The few times she saw it parked out front, he didn't drop by the main house. Instead, he holed up in the bungalow, burning the midnight oil, so to speak. By Wednesday, she began leaving muffins, yogurt, fruit, and juice in a cooler on his patio table, so he wouldn't go without breakfast in the mornings. Thursday evening, when she replaced the contents with something fresh, there was a note resting inside.

"Mahalo," it read.

Lani crinkled the paper in her hand, scrunching it into a ball. How hard would it have been to write *Mahalo Lani*? He had to know it was her. She looked around, seeing a dark bungalow, a missing Subaru, and an empty hammock. A knot of loneliness clenched her stomach, feeling like a foreshadowing of what was to come.

Absence makes the heart grow fonder, came the thought.

Lani was living proof of that. Instead of missing Easton less, she missed him more and more and more. By Friday morning, she was ready to lounge in his hammock and not leave until he showed his face.

But she didn't. She booked a reservation, cleaned, scrubbed, and even weeded an area of the lawn that grew the most noxious of weeds, just because it was close to the bungalow. But no Easton.

When Friday evening finally rolled around, Lani became desperate for a diversion and asked Pearl to teach her how to play Mahjong. Puna joined in as well, and the three of them were out on the main lanai at dusk, enjoying the refreshing evening breeze, when Easton drove in. A car door slammed, the headlights blinked on and off, and he waved and called out "Aloha" on his way to the bungalow before disappearing inside.

Lani scowled at the tiles, frustrated with the game and frustrated with Easton. He'd practically kissed *her,* not the other way around—actually, not practically, he *had* kissed her. So why was he the one doing the avoiding? Was this how it would be the rest of the summer—him coming and going, waving, leaving polite notes, then sneaking away at the end of it all, just to avoid saying goodbye?

An annoying voice in the back of her mind whispered, *Isn't this what you wanted?*

Maybe once, but not anymore. What Lani wanted now was for him to look at her in that tender way he'd looked at her before he kissed her. She wanted to feel his touch, smell his clean, sporty scent, and hear his distinctive voice. And she wanted him to tell his sweet little niece that he wouldn't be home as soon as he'd promised, that he'd met someone special, someone different than all the other girls he'd met before.

But deep down, Lani knew that if Easton's feelings ran half as deep as hers, he wouldn't have wasted another week of the short amount of time they had left avoiding her.

"That boy is *lolo*," said Puna, shaking her head.

"You can say that again," muttered Lani before she reconsidered her words. She regretted them the moment the gleam appeared in her grandmother's eyes. "I was talking about the boy at the market today," Lani rushed to say. "The one who miscounted my change."

"You're not much better." Puna pointed a wrinkly finger at her, making Lani's frown lines deepen. "What you need to do is give up on this game, march up that hill, and tell that boy what you're really thinking."

"No. What I need to do is match two tiles. Who invented this game, anyway? It's awful."

"I don't think it's the game that's awful." Puna said the words under her breath, and Lani wasn't sure she'd heard right.

"What did you just say?"

"Nothing."

Lani glared at her grandmother. "That's what I thought."

Pearl's lips lifted into her usual serene smile that further annoyed Lani. It was like everyone around her knew something she didn't, and she was tired of feeling like she was missing something. Or more specifically, some*one*.

Stop thinking about Easton! she yelled at herself. *Focus on the game instead.*

Lani scanned the tiles for the umpteenth time and, at last, found a match.

"Aha!" She proceeded to collect the two tiles, only to be halted by a quiet comment from Pearl.

"Are you sure those are a match?"

Lani looked closer and noticed there was one less black line on one, but she refused to let one little line stop her. "I think someone just drew on this one with marker. It's definitely a match." She placed the tiles in front of her and shot Puna a look that said, *Go ahead and try to challenge me on this. I dare you.*

Pearl chuckled and clasped her fingers together. "I think something is eating at you, Lani."

"You're just now noticing?" said Puna as she retrieved Lani's tiles and put them back in play. The bright orange of her muumuu usually made Lani smile. Today, it made her wish she'd worn sunglasses.

"I'm good," said Lani, trying to convince herself as well. "Great, in fact. Never been better."

"Psh," said Puna. "If you're great, than I'm a hibiscus."

"You do sort of look like one," countered Lani, looking at her dress.

Puna ignored her. "I'm telling you, go talk to that boy. It's the only way you're going to feel better."

Lani retrieved the two tiles that were almost a match and placed them in front of her. "What good will that do? Not all of us get that fairytale romance like you had, Puna. In four weeks, Easton will be gone forever, and I will still be here."

Her heart would crack in half when that day came, and half again every day thereafter until there was nothing left but confetti.

Maybe she could throw herself a party with it.

Tired of the game—and conversation—Lani was ready to make up an excuse about needing to clean something when she noticed Easton coming their way. Her body tensed, her heart thundered, and her breathing became irregular. It was like she'd involuntarily given him control of more than just her heart. Her entire being responded to him, which was ridiculous. No one should have that much control over a person.

Yes, it was definitely past time to clean something. Lani pushed her chair back, ready to pretend like she hadn't seen him and flee.

"Aloha," he called, making any pretense impossible. "Long time no see." He jogged the rest of the way to greet them and was soon standing behind Lani.

"That's not a match," he felt the need to point out. His arm brushed her cheek as he pointed to the two tiles resting in front of her.

"According to Lani, someone drew an extra line on that one," said Puna. "Would you care to join us, Easton?"

Lani's heart was about to skitter right out of her chest, so she pushed her chair to the side. "You can take my place. I need to . . . um . . ." Her mind went completely blank. She'd had the perfect excuse moments before. What was it, again?

"Clean the kitchen?" offered Pearl.

"Yes, that's right. I need to clean the kitchen." Lani stood and ran her sweating palms across the front of her denim shorts. "If you'll excuse me."

"I'll help," Easton offered unhelpfully.

"No," said Lani. "You can't. You're a guest."

"And if a guest would like to help clean the kitchen, you should let him," Puna added. "It's good customer service to allow them to do what they want."

Her grandmother had multiple sides to her personality. Sweet, enthusiastic, hard-working, and infuriating. Now, she was being the latter.

"Mahalo for the offer," said Lani to Easton. "But it won't take me long."

"Then I'll keep you company while you work."

No wonder Puna liked Easton so well. He could be just as infuriating. Lani threw up her hands. "Fine. If you really want to spend more of your vacation time cleaning, then be my *guest*."

"Hey, you're punny," said Easton with a smile that turned Lani's knees to jelly. She quickly strode inside, wondering about the state of her mental health. Five minutes ago, she couldn't wait to see him again, and now it was all she could do to get away from him.

He followed behind, pausing on the threshold to the kitchen. "It looks clean to me."

Lani continued to the fridge and pulled it open. "This isn't."

"You're going to clean out the fridge on a Friday night?"

"That's exactly what I'm going to do."

He followed again, stopping behind her. Even though he didn't touch her, she could feel the warmth radiating from his body, along with a tickle on her neck from his breath. She should have worn her hair down today.

"Looks clean and organized to me," he said.

"That's because you're a man, and men are immune to clutter."

"Or maybe we just don't obsess about stuff that doesn't really matter."

Lani frowned and grabbed a few Tupperware containers and set them on the counter. Then she reached for the eggs, but Easton took her arm instead, pulling her gently to the side. Then he returned the Tupperware containers to the shelf and closed the door, resting his back against it and folding his arms as he studied her.

"You've been avoiding me again."

"No. You've been avoiding *me*," she said. "Which is fine because I want to be avoided." Actually, what she really wanted was to *want* to want to be avoided.

He continued to watch her, and Lani felt like someone had stapled her flip-flops to the floor. She couldn't run away, back away, or even look away. Everything about him became magnetic, pulling her body closer to his.

"Why did you go to Costco on Monday?" he asked.

She swallowed. "Supplies. We were out of . . . supplies."

"According to Cora, you only need to do a supply run about once a month."

"Summers are busier."

He pushed away from the fridge and approached her. "Know what I think? I think you went on a four-hour excursion to get away from me."

Her body trembling, Lani took a step back and bumped into the island. It suddenly felt closer to the fridge than normal. If there was something Lani hated more than not having control over her emotions, it was being put on the spot like this.

"I . . . I . . ." The emotional exhaustion was taking its toll. She didn't want to play this game anymore. He knew how she felt about closed doors and short-term relationships, so why was he inching closer, asking questions he already knew the answers to, when Lani had no clue what he wanted from her.

"You're not playing fair," she blurted. "You know exactly what I think and where I stand, but you never reciprocate. I have no idea what you're thinking. All I know is that you're leaving in four weeks and hate goodbyes. So yeah, I was avoiding you. I'm still trying to avoid you. In fact, I think Puna's calling my name." Lani practically raced back to the lanai, only to stop short in the doorway.

The sky was darker now, and Puna, Pearl, and the stupid Mahjong game had disappeared. The table and chairs had been pushed to the side, and instead of the four can lights that usually lit the space, a strand of white lights had been woven around the railing. Even worse, soft music played from somewhere.

She backed away and bumped into Easton.

With his hands on her shoulders, he steadied her. Then he chuckled. "I think Cora and Pearl are trying to tell us something," he said in her ear.

Without answering, Lani pulled free, determined to find the source of the music and get rid of it. But it seemed to be coming from all around her, as though there were speakers in every room. But there weren't. The only speakers in the house were a small set she plugged her phone into when she cleaned or worked. Lani was beginning to feel like she was losing her mind.

Easton leaned against the doorway, watching her with an amused expression.

"Do you hear that?" Lani looked around.

"Hear what?"

She *was* going crazy. *Easton* had driven her crazy.

"Are you talking about the music?" he asked.

"Yes, I'm talking about the music. Where's it coming from?" She looked around again, trying to figure it out. She hadn't heard the music until she'd reached this point, but now, everywhere she walked—down the hall and back again—the volume sounded exactly the same.

"I'm going insane," she murmured out loud.

Easton slipped his hand into hers and gently pulled her out to the lanai. "We should dance."

"I don't want to dance." Lani wished she meant it. But his shoulders and arms looked so heavenly. How she'd love to walk into them, rest her whirring head against his neck, and forget about all the things that didn't make sense.

"Will you dance with me, Lani?" he asked, his voice quiet.

Her chest rose and fell with each heavy breath, and her fingers tingled where he touched them. "Why?" she asked, needing something from him. Anything.

"Because I've missed you. Because I like to be near you. And because I don't want all of Pearl and Cora's work to be wasted." He paused, giving her hand a squeeze. "Please? Just one dance?"

She found herself being pulled into his arms, and the moment she felt them around her, she knew she was a goner. Her skin burned where he touched her, and a thousand sensations rippled across her, as though she'd been sprinkled with fairy dust. Lani had never felt so light and shivery or warm and wonderful.

"I've Got You Under My Skin" by Frank Sinatra floated from somewhere, and Easton kicked off his sandals and tucked her close against him, keeping one of her hands in his. His other arm circled her back, and her free hand settled on his shoulder. She relaxed against him, and her mind drained of everything but him. As the last of the dusk melted away, all that remained was a speckling of little white lights. It was magical—a moment Lani knew would be seared into her memory forever.

"What's happening?" she whispered.

"It's called dancing," he whispered back. "Just go with it."

She did. Lani let him spin her around, pull her close, and sway. Song after song floated from somewhere, all from a different time and place. Nat King Cole, Bing Crosby, Elvis, and Ella Fitzgerald. She fell under the spell of the music, the lights . . . Easton. At one point, he led her down the steps and out onto the lawn, and somehow the music followed.

As a Fred Astaire song came to a close, Easton dipped Lani down low, then brought her up slowly. "Are you going to stop avoiding me now?"

She searched his eyes, needing to know what he was feeling and thinking and hoping for. "What do you want?"

"To spend time with you, talk to you, dance with you, and kiss you. I want to see what can happen."

In and out she breathed, her thoughts a foggy mass. "What *can* happen?" she asked, unclear about the possibilities.

"That's what I'd like to find out." His palms framed her face, and his thumb slid along her jaw. "All I know is that I want more moments like this. A lot more."

Lani trembled under his touch. More than anything she wanted to forget about the four-week deadline, allow herself to fall completely under his spell, and, like he said, see what happened. But something held her back—something she needed to know before she could put any trust in him.

"If nothing . . . happens," she said. "Will your heart break too? Or is mine the only one at risk here?"

The color of his eyes deepened as they searched hers. "I'm scared too, Lani. But I'm also hopeful. I don't know whether or not things will work out in the long run, but I want them to, and I know I'll be hurt if they don't. The truth is, I never want to say goodbye to you—and not because I avoid goodbyes like the plague—but because I want to keep saying aloha and good night and good morning and—"

Lani pulled his head toward her and pressed her lips to his. They were warm, moist, and heavenly, just like she knew they would be. He froze for a split second, and then he was kissing her back. His hands moved from her face to around her shoulders, and he crushed her against him, working his mouth over hers like an expert.

A million sensations cascaded over Lani, awakening every part of her. She felt strong and weak, secure and vulnerable, thrilled and fearful. Every emotion had its opposite, and yet they somehow worked together, making her feel more alive than she'd ever felt before.

This is what it feels like to soar, she thought.

His hands returned to her face, and the kiss became slower and more deliberate, easing her out of a beautiful dream. Then he broke free and pulled her tight against him, burying his face in her hair. His chest rose and fell, and a song faded in—one Lani had never heard before. She struggled to catch her breath and bring herself back to reality.

Easton shifted positions and his forehead touched hers, while his palms still cradled her face.

"Will you spend tomorrow with me?" he breathed.

"Yes."

Her answer made him smile, and he leaned in for one last kiss before he backed away, keeping hold of one of her hands until it was out of reach. A hint of laughter rumbled in his voice when he said, "Sweet dreams."

Lani smiled as she floated back inside. From the window just inside the door, she watched him climb the rest of the hill to the bungalow and glance over his shoulder before disappearing inside. Only then did she realize she couldn't hear the music any longer.

chapter 17

Easton was at breakfast early the next morning. Lani paused before opening the door and willed her heart not to skip too many beats when she saw him take a seat next to Pearl. Freshly shaven, he looked handsome and confident and oh so kissable. She didn't know what the plans were for the day, but she'd gotten up with the sun to catch up on emails and other correspondence so she could be ready to go whenever he was.

Two women in their early-thirties were staying for two days. They were sitting at an adjacent table wearing lace cover-ups over brightly-colored bikinis. They both kept glancing at Easton, looking him over like he was a decadent chocolate dessert in the middle of a vegetable buffet. But Easton didn't notice, or pretended not to notice, and kept his attention focused on Pearl.

Lani's heart double-skipped at that.

She opened the door and walked out on the patio. He looked her way and smiled, his eyes warm and focused on her. She smiled back and said, "Aloha" as she handed a steaming mug of cocoa to Pearl.

"Mahalo, Lani," said Pearl.

Lani was about to make her way back to the kitchen when Easton grabbed her hand and pulled her in for a quick kiss—in front of everyone.

Lani blushed, the women averted their gazes, Pearl smiled, and Easton said, "How soon can l steal you away?"

"As soon as breakfast is cleaned up. How does oatmeal sound this morning?"

"Great."

Lani turned to the other table. "What about you, ladies? Would you like some oatmeal as well, or I can whip up an omelet or—"

"Two omelets would be great," said the one wearing a large-brimmed hat. "All egg whites, with a little salt and pepper and no cheese."

"Speak for yourself," said the freckled brunette. "I'll take two whole eggs with lots of cheese in mine. If that's not too much trouble."

"But what about—" started her friend.

"We're on vacation, Leah. This is the reason we went on that horrible diet in the first place—so we could enjoy ourselves in Hawaii. Remember?"

Her friend seemed to waffle for a moment before she nodded in agreement. "You're right. Load mine up with cheese as well."

"Still egg-whites only?" Lani clarified.

More hesitation. Then resolve. "Yes. I can't bring myself to go off the diet cold turkey, not after all my hard work."

Lani laughed, liking the two women despite the fact they'd eyed Easton earlier. Who could blame them, really? Lani couldn't keep her eyes off him either.

She returned to the kitchen and found Puna talking to Ahe, who had just arrived with some fresh catch. He plopped them on the counter and wiped his forearm against his forehead before adjusting his baseball cap. His dark hair curled from beneath it.

"I got some tuna and snapper today," he said with pride.

Lani couldn't resist grabbing his shoulders and giving him a peck on the cheek. Snapper was her favorite. "Mahalo, Ahe. I'll be making bread tomorrow to return the favor. Any requests?"

"Banana, honey oat, pumpkin, that kind with cinnamon and raisons, and—"

"Whoa. I'm sorry I asked." She laughed. "I meant one request. Not ten."

He grinned then rubbed the scruff on his chin with his fingers. "Honey oat."

"Honey oat it is, assuming I have any oats left. Easton's a fan of oatmeal, so I'm going through it a lot quicker these days."

His grin vanished, replaced by a scowl. "When does that haole leave again?"

Lani gave him a look that said *Don't start.* Then she put the tuna in the freezer and the snapper in the fridge. Maybe she'd invite Easton to enjoy it with them tonight. "I thought you were beginning to like him."

The scowl remained. "He's okay."

Puna laughed. "I think that's a compliment coming from Ahe."

"There's something about him I don't trust," he added. "He's too . . . something. It's like he's hiding something."

Feeling suddenly defensive, Lani said, "Maybe if you got to know him like we do you wouldn't feel that way."

"And everyone hides things," added Puna, seemingly

unconcerned. She pulled a ball of dough from the refrigerator and began rolling it out on the island. "I guarantee even you have secrets, Ahe."

He shifted positions and looked away, making no comment.

"Nobody's perfect," she continued. "You just have to find someone whose perfections you love and imperfections you can live with." Her lips lifted into a smile as she worked. "Kadir, bless his heart, used to forget about everything. My birthday, our anniversary, dinner plans, *his* birthday." She laughed at that. "But he never forgot me or anyone else. When I needed him, he was there, and I never doubted his love for me."

Lani's heart warmed. She loved that Puna now spoke about her grandfather without reserve. It was yet another thing she would always be grateful to Easton for—that he'd unwittingly opened a door Lani had always thought would be barricaded closed.

Ahe watched Lani with a look of worry. "Are you and the haole . . .?"

She knew what he was asking, and the question hung between them like the catch of the day gone bad. Lani didn't want to hurt her friend, but she didn't want to lie to him either. She flipped one finished omelet onto a plate and shoved it into the microwave to stay warm while she cooked the other.

"I don't know," she said quietly. "I think we might be, but I'm not sure yet."

Silence. Ahe was no longer looking at her. He didn't appear to be looking at anything really, just staring. Lani didn't know what else to say. She felt like she'd committed a crime she hadn't meant to commit, but it couldn't be helped. And now she was left with the consequences.

Puna slapped her hands together to rid them of some excess flour. "Are those omelets ready yet? I'll take them out, if you'd like."

Lani scooped up the second omelet, slid it onto the plate and handed both to Puna. "This is for the one wearing a hat."

Puna nodded and swept out of the kitchen with her purple muumuu swaying around her.

Lani dumped some oatmeal into the now-boiling water and began to stir. One Mississippi, two Mississsippi, three Mississippi—

"How about we spend today together," Ahe said. "We can surf, dive, fish, and—"

"I can't. I'm sorry," she said, her heart breaking for him. She hated this aspect about love—the unfairness of it all. First Derek and now Ahe. Why did their feelings have to go deeper than friendship? Why hadn't hers? Why did good people have to get hurt?

When Lani thought about it, it was miraculous that two people of like minds and feelings ever found each other. Of all the people in the world who weren't right for you, what were the odds of finding someone who was?

Slim.

Ahe planted his palms on the counter and leaned in close. "You sure you want to fall for a haole?"

She shut off the heat and stared at the churning oatmeal. "You're forgetting that I'm a haole too," she said quietly.

He lifted her chin to look at him and shook his head, his expression vulnerable and sad. "You've never been a haole to me."

No, no, no, she wanted to scream. *Why this, why now, why him?* Ahe had given up so much for the people he cared about—so much for her. She couldn't stand the thought of making him suffer. But this wasn't something that could be made right with a loaf of bread or even a hundred loaves. It went deeper than she knew how to fix.

And it felt so wrong.

Tears leaked from the corner of her eyes, and she pressed them closed. Ahe's hand left her face, and he pulled her into a burly hug.

"It's okay, *sistah*. You can't make your feelings be what they aren't. Believe me, I know." Then he kissed her forehead, let her go, and walked out the side door, letting the screen door slam shut behind him.

Lani tried to control her composure, but it began to crumble, breaking into pieces around her. Her body trembled, and the tears came more freely.

"Everything okay?" came Pearl's soft voice from the doorway.

Lani sniffed and shook her head, turning to look at the sweet woman. "I hurt Ahe, Pearl. I didn't mean to, but I did, and now . . . I don't know how to make it right."

Pearl set down her empty mug and moved forward, clasping Lani by the shoulders. She seemed to know exactly what Lani was talking about. "I once met a woman who told me there's a lid for every bucket, regardless of its shape, color and size. I believe that. You need to believe that. When the time is right, Ahe will find his match, and so will Derek. I promise you that."

Somehow, Lani believed it. Coming from Pearl, it was impossible not to. She was like an angel who seemed to know the best outcome and helped people find their way. Her coming here and staying here didn't feel like happenstance anymore. It felt more like Providence.

"Mahalo, Pearl. For everything."

She patted Lani's arm and offered a smile. "I think my vacation here is about over. I will be checking out next week."

Lani's composure cracked all over again, but she nodded through her tears anyway. "We'll miss you."

"And I you." Pearl's hands dropped to her side, and she looked around the kitchen, spotting the rolled out dough on the island.

"What is Cora doing here?"

"I think she's making her amazing coconut cream pie. Please say you'll join us for dinner tonight."

"I would love to."

"What about me?" said Easton from the doorway. "Am I invited too? Or will dinner be like breakfast where I'm left alone on the lanai, forgotten?"

Lani laughed, wiping the last of her tears away. "I'm sorry. I have your oatmeal right here."

She turned to lift the pan off the stove, and Easton's arms came around her waist from behind. He kissed a sensitive area on her neck and murmured, "Everything okay?"

"Yes."

"It shouldn't be. You forgot to invite me to dinner."

"Did I?" Warm and light feelings began to chase out the sadness.

"Yes."

"I'm sorry."

He shifted to the side and looked at her profile for a moment before he poked her in the ribs.

She squirmed away, laughing as Puna breezed in and picked up her rolling pin without a word. Lani noticed that Pearl was no longer in the room. She must have slipped out.

Easton's lips lifted into a sly smile, and he folded his arms, his gaze trained on Lani. "Hey, Cora, whatcha making?"

"A coconut cream pie."

"Mmm . . . I love coconut cream pies."

"Then you should join us for dinner. We have plenty."

The look in his eyes changed from amused to triumphant, and his grin widened. "I would love to. Mahalo." Then he reached past Lani to pick up the pot of oatmeal and began preparing it himself.

Fighting back a smile, Lani passed him the container of brown sugar and murmured, "I was going to invite you eventually."

"I know. But now I don't have to grovel."

She smiled and gave him a quick peck on the lips. "Too bad. I think it's pretty endearing when you do."

chapter 18 ❀

Easton shoved a box of granola bars into his backpack and zipped it closed. His plan for the day included a day trip along the lesser-traveled southeastern side of Maui. Other than packing some snacks and drinks, that's how he worked. Pick a direction and see where it took him, like a real-life choose-your-own-adventure. No wonder he liked those books so much as a kid.

But would Lani be game?

As soon as he told her what he had in mind, Easton had his answer. She peeked into his backpack full of snacks and gave him a pained look.

"Do you want a grumpy date or a happy date?" she asked.

"Um . . . happy?"

"Then I'll be right back." Fifteen minutes later, she returned with a small cooler loaded with freshly made sandwiches and fruit. Her explanation: "I like junk food just as much as the next person, but if that's all I eat—or if I go too long without eating—I become Scrooge."

Easton grinned, enjoying her honesty, initiative, and the adorable way she looked in a baseball hat with her hair pulled back.

"Good to know," he said. "Anything else make you grumpy that I should know about?"

She watched him for a moment before she cocked her head to the side. "Yeah. Guests who leave without saying goodbye." Even though she'd said it in a teasing way, there was an underlying distrust in her eyes. *If this doesn't work out, is that how we'll part ways?*

From the get-go, Lani had made it pretty clear to Easton where he stood with her. At first, it was at arms' length. Then a polite distance away. Now it was much closer. But until she trusted him completely, he wasn't where he wanted to be.

"I don't . . ." Easton's voice trailed off. Sharing his innermost thoughts had never come easily to him. He preferred to keep them off the table and out of the limelight. But if he continued to do that, things would never progress between them, and he was finally ready for them to go somewhere.

He tried again. "You know I don't want it to come to that, but if it does, I promise that I will say goodbye to you."

"In person?"

He chuckled. "The things you ask of me."

The corners of her lips tugged up, but her expression remained sad. "It's never easy to say goodbye to someone you care about, but better a real goodbye than nothing."

Easton wasn't so sure he agreed with her, but a promise was a promise. He slung his arm around her shoulders and steered her toward his car. "Enough about goodbyes. What do you say about getting out of here?"

"I say, let's go."

Easton pulled her close and kissed her on the forehead.

Then they tossed their stuff in the trunk and off they went. Not long after they passed the pools of Ohe'o, Easton pulled off the side of the road at every shoulder they came across. Once out of the car, they'd either hike up the mountain a ways or pick their way down to the rustic coastline. Each place they stopped, they stumbled across something different and beautiful, like a charming little waterfall or a rocky and barren beach with 270-degree views. They found a sea turtle lounging in a small cove, a little yellow bird tweeting from a low branch in a tree, and a large brown spider that made Lani leap onto Easton's back.

"I hate spiders, I hate spiders, I hate them," she whimpered as he carried her away.

Easton smiled, content to keep her arms around his neck. "I take it spiders are another thing that make you grumpy?"

"Not so much grumpy as . . . they make me feel like I'm covered in ants," she said with a shiver.

"Don't worry. I'll save you." He carried her a little farther before setting her down. "You okay now?"

She rubbed her hands together and watched him warily. "You're thinking I'm the world's biggest wuss right now, aren't you?"

He grinned and stole a quick kiss, saying, "Well, the prettiest wuss anyway." Then he tucked some errant hair behind her ear and reached for her hand, walking with her the rest of the way to the car. At the next beach, they stopped for lunch.

Easton located a large boulder to sit on, and Lani pulled out the sandwiches she'd made and handed him one. He took a bite and nudged her shoulder with his. "You are an amazing cook. Even your sandwiches taste better than any deli's I've had before."

She smiled. "Mahalo, but I think you're just really hungry."

"No. I'm telling you, these are amazing. Did you make these rolls?"

"Yes, but any talent I have with baking I owe to one of my college roommates. Her parents owned a small bakery, and she taught me how to make everything from doughnuts to bread bowls and pastries. She even shared all her family's secret recipes, making me promise I wouldn't pass them along to anyone else. It's probably why everyone here loves my breads so much—because I can't share the recipes."

He shot her a sidelong glance. "You've never given one of those recipes to anyone?"

She shook her head. "I made a promise I wouldn't."

"Not even Cora?"

Lani shrugged. "I keep them in a small box in the kitchen cupboard, so I suppose she could use them if she wanted, but she never does. She leaves all the baking to me."

"What about your future husband? Would you share them with him?"

"I would have to call my friend and ask her first," Lani teased, though Easton got the feeling she really would.

He took another bite of his sandwich and let his gaze travel across the turquoise and azure blue waters. The sea churned up white cap after white cap, looking as unsteady as he suddenly felt. His father had always advised him to marry above him—to find a woman who would inspire him to be a better person—but now that he'd met Lani, he couldn't help but wonder if she was too far above him.

"What else do you like to do besides bake, hike, sing, surf, and manage a B&B?" he asked. "Do you play an instrument?"

"I'm only so-so on the piano, and I took flute lessons

one year in high school before I decided it wasn't for me. I preferred singing to playing. What about you?"

"I can strum about five chords on the guitar and that's it," he said. "Play any organized sports?"

"Volleyball and tennis. You?"

"Nope." He shook his head. "I mean, I like sports and everything, I just hated the organized form of them."

"Why?"

Easton took the last bite of his sandwich and brushed the crumbs from his hands. "I wanted to play what I felt like playing at the moment, and the thought of doing the same thing every day for months at a time always made me want to croak. I'm pretty sure my parents used to worry I had no drive or ambition and would never be able to find a career I liked for more than a few weeks."

Lani pulled her knees to her chest and studied him. "How did you handle school?"

"I always enjoyed learning, but hated the classroom setting. After high school, my parents didn't push college on me, for which I was grateful, though I did take several writing classes, along with a few others that interested me, and I eventually earned enough credits for an Associate's, but that's it. In case you haven't gathered, I'm more of a hands-on guy."

Worry lines creased Lani's brow. "I take it you're not interested in ever settling down?"

It was a question his parents and sisters had all asked him, a question voiced by a few of the women he'd dated. Easton's answer had always been the same. Nope. But Lani was making him reconsider several things, especially his future. If there was one thing he was coming to know for certain, it was that he wanted her in it. If that meant compromising some things, he was okay with that. But he couldn't compromise everything. Easton would never be happy working a nine-to-five job or living year-round in a suburb with a fenced-in yard and neighbors whose faces never changed.

"I wouldn't mind having a home base, so to speak," he said. "But I'll always want to travel and see new places, cultures, and people. It's my way of learning and progressing. Without it, I'd feel . . . I don't know . . . stagnant, I guess."

From the corner of his eye, Easton watched Lani, wondering what she thought about him after all this. Was she the sort of person who needed more than just a home base? Did she need constancy and stability and the kind of regular life that he could never offer?

That was a wild card—one of the things that could lead to a goodbye.

He held his breath, waiting for her to say something. Anything. When a full minute passed and she didn't, he forced himself to ask the scariest question he'd ever asked. "Is that a deal-breaker for you?"

Her eyes flew to his and widened in surprise. "I didn't realize we were making a deal."

"We aren't, exactly. I just . . ." He scratched the back of his neck, wishing that conversations like this never had to take place. Why couldn't they just read each other's minds? It would make everything so much easier.

"Just what?" she asked.

He shifted positions to face her. "When I said before that I didn't want to say goodbye, that wasn't a lie. I really don't. But I can't offer you a typical life. So even though we're not officially making deals yet, I need to know whether or not a deal is even possible with you."

She blinked. Once. Twice. Three times. And then she swallowed and looked down at her fingers that were rolling a leaf into a tight cylinder. Easton gently rescued the leaf before capturing her hand in his, prodding her to look at him.

"What are you thinking, Lani?"

She swallowed again. "That a home base sounds nice. As does seeing new places. I'm just wondering about what I would do or how I'd fit into that lifestyle."

Easton let out the breath he'd been holding and smiled. A life with her wasn't just a pipe dream. They were talking about reality here—or, an almost-reality. "Hypothetically speaking," he said, running his fingers through hers, "what if the home base was here, where you have a job that you like and you're good at? Then when we're away, maybe you can . . . I don't know, invest in a traveling bakery?"

She laughed and shook her head. "I'd never want to turn baking into a career, but if it really comes to that, I'm sure I can come up with something. But what about your family? You sound so close and—"

"They'll have to understand that my visits home will be fewer and further between, and I think they will if it means welcoming a new member of the family. And I'm pretty positive they won't mind coming to visit us in Maui every once in a while."

"We'll have a great place for them to stay."

He liked her use of we. "Yes, we will."

"I'll have to warn Ahe about the possibility of more haoles coming," she teased.

Easton chuckled. "I'll make sure to be far away when you have that conversation with him."

"That's probably a good idea. Especially consider-ing . . ." Her voice trailed off, and she bit her lower lip, saying nothing more.

"Considering he's in love with you, too?"

Her eyes flew to his. "Too?" she whispered.

Easton leaned in close, pausing with his mouth touching the area near her ear and above her jaw. She smelled like apples and wildflowers and sunshine. He breathed her in, his muscles pulsating with an energy he'd never felt before. In that moment, he saw clarity. A life with Lani at his side was a life he wanted more than anything else.

"Too," he murmured. And then he kissed her. Her breath hitched, and after a moment's pause her lips responded, moving across his, igniting a fire every place they touched. Their first real kiss had been one of desire—a long-awaited reward for something Easton had wanted to do since the day he'd laid eyes on her. This kiss, on the other hand, was one of discovery. He took his time, paying attention to the ripples in her lips, the smile lines at the corner of her mouth, and the indent at the peak of her upper lip. His hands cupped her face as he memorized the slope of her jaw and cheekbone, the softness of her skin, her ear . . . He pushed her hat from her head and slid his fingers into her silky hair, feeling the contours of her head.

Everything about Lani moved him, lifted him, touched him. She softened his hard edges, filled his cracks, and made him believe in something greater and better. This was why people left the door open, why they stayed, why they committed, why they held on tight and never let go.

Until now, Easton had never understood.

His hands returned to her face, and he kissed her once, twice, three times, then slowly pulled back. His heart hammered, his breath came in quick spurts, and everything around him seemed to take on a surreal glow. It reminded him of his writing. Usually, the articles or posts he wrote required tweaking and multiple revisions. But every so often, something amazing happened. He'd feel a release in his mind and beautiful words would flow down through his fingertips and appear on the screen—ordinary words that came together in an extraordinary way. Words that invoked clarity, feeling, and power. No tweaking or revisions were needed. They were just . . . right.

That's what it felt like now. Right.

"I love you, too," she said softly.

Easton slid behind her and pulled her tight against him, tucking his arms around her waist. The scent of the sand and sea mixed with the apples and wildflowers of her hair, and a light breeze swept across his neck. Only then did he notice that gloomy, gray clouds had taken over the sky, blocking out the sunlight.

And then a raindrop fell from the sky and landed on his nose.

chapter 19

fter Friday, Lani felt like constantly skipping and dancing, twirling and singing. She'd never felt so light on her feet or glorious. She awoke early on Saturday, ready to work fast and hard so she could spend whatever time was left with Easton. When a grumpy bachelor checked in around noon, she didn't bat an eye when he felt the need to point out every crack in the sidewalk, the few weeds in a flower bed they passed, the faded patio furniture, the squeak of the screen door, and the inefficient layout of the front room.

Lani could have argued with him about everything. The cracks gave the walkways character. The "weeds" were actually sensitive plants—put there on purpose for the guests to enjoy. The door squeaked and the furniture had faded because of the rain, humidity, and sun—three of the things that made Maui the paradise it was. And the furniture had been arranged like that so guests could enjoy the views from the two large windows.

But she didn't say a thing. A man who noticed thorns instead of roses *wanted* to see the thorns. So she'd oiled the door, walked past the faded patio furniture and over the cracks in the walkway, touched the leaves of the sensitive plants and smiled when they curled together.

That afternoon, instead of snorkeling and kayaking like they'd planned, Lani and Easton helped Maaike's family pick papayas and cabbages for the roadside stand they owned. Her father had fallen ill, and her mother had taken him to the doctor. With her two brothers out of town, she needed help. So Lani and Easton changed their plans and their clothes and drove to Maaike's instead. Easton didn't complain at all. He simply dug in and got to work like he had the day the Akua room had been torn apart.

After spending the majority of the afternoon hunched over cabbage plants and climbing rickety ladders, they smelled like earth and papayas and looked worse. But Lani didn't care. She wrapped her arms around Easton's waist and kissed a smudge on his cheek.

"If I didn't already love you, I would after today," she said. "Mahalo."

He brushed her hair from her face. "You seem to like this kind of work."

She made a face. "Picking produce? I don't think so."

"I meant helping someone out."

"Oh. Well, yeah, that's easy to like." Lani kept her arm around his waist as they walked toward the car. "The people here are kind and grateful and so generous that when an opportunity comes along to give something back, it feels more like a blessing than work."

He nodded and kissed the top of her head. "I know what you mean."

They arrived at the car, and he opened the door for her.

"What do you say we grab a sandwich in town and stop at Hamoa to wash off in the ocean?"

"But I didn't bring my suit."

He shrugged. "You didn't have your suit yesterday either, but we still had fun in the rain."

He was right. The storm had created a muddy mess of everything—the road, mountains, beaches—but they'd continued their jaunt around the south side of the island regardless, only having to free the car from mud twice. By the time they pulled in that night, they were soggy and the car was filthy, and yet Lani had never had such a perfect day. It had been an adventure—the beginning of many, she hoped.

By the time Sunday evening rolled around, they'd talked of her flying to Boston with him to meet his family and planned to approach Puna about making the bungalow their home between travels. Everything was falling into place in a way that Lani had never imagined it could.

"You're glowing," Puna commented on Sunday afternoon as they relaxed in the front room. Easton had left moments before to place his weekly FaceTime call to his parents and family. He'd invited Lani to come along so she could "meet" everyone, but she'd declined, saying she'd rather wait and do it in person, not through a small phone screen with a connection that could drop off at any moment.

So he'd left, and Lani began rifling through the small stack of DVDs she'd brought with her from the states, trying to find a good movie to watch.

"You should have gone with him," said Puna, swaying back and forth in her favorite rocking chair, her pink and green muumuu splashing around her ankles. Her hands rested across her ample stomach, and her eyes were closed.

"I would feel awkward. What would I say? Hi, I'm Lani. Your son hasn't mentioned me to you yet because everything is happening so fast, but we're thinking about spending the rest of our lives together. I hope that's okay. By the way, can you see me? Or, at least my nose?" Lani glanced at the movie she held then returned it to the basket. Nothing sounded good. "Don't make me feel guilty for not going with him."

Puna continued to rock. "I just know if it were my son, I'd want to meet you. And your nose is lovely, dear. Don't be ashamed of it."

Lani laughed. "You're only saying that because I got your nose. But you're right, it is a good nose."

Eyes still closed, Puna waved a hand dismissively. "Go. Meet the parents. Show them the treasure their son has found in Hāna."

"I think the real treasure found me," said Lani.

"You can tell them that too."

Lani's heart softened. Easton had looked a little disappointed when she'd passed on his invitation, so maybe she should go. Slowly, she pushed the basket back under the TV and rose to kiss Puna on her wrinkled cheek. "You've convinced me. I'll go. Not because I want to but because I've learned to trust your wisdom."

"Flatterer." But her mouth lifted into a smile nonetheless.

"Be back soon." Lani took the purple throw off the couch and tucked it around her grandmother before treading lightly across the floor and out the door, closing it softly behind her. She breathed in the fragrant white orchids as she passed them and lifted her gaze to the late afternoon sky, where a speckling of clouds shaded her from the sun.

As she climbed the hill, Easton's low-murmuring voice grew in volume. Through the open window, she could see

that he sat in an armchair with his back to her, and as soon as she reached the stairs of the lanai, she could hear him clearly—along with the people he spoke with. She paused to listen as she gathered her courage to knock on his door.

"Caleb," Easton's voice teased, "I hate to break it to you, but I can still see you."

"No you can't!" a little boy's voice bellowed. "I've got my invisible coat on."

"You mean your invisibility cloak."

"Yes!"

"Well, it's not working. You're wearing a red and blue plaid shirt and a cheeky smile. You should tell your mom to get you a real cloak."

"They don't have real ones," he pouted.

"Then you should tell your mom to get you a puppy instead. You can name it Harry or Ron or . . ."

"Dumbledorf!" Caleb exclaimed. Footsteps pattered away and his voice grew fainter as he called, "Mom! Mom! Mom!"

A moment later, a woman's voice bellowed from farther away. "Thanks a lot, East."

Feminine and masculine laughter sounded before a woman took control of the conversation.

"What day are you flying home again? You told me a few weeks ago, but I didn't have my calendar with me and can't remember now," she said.

"Um . . ." Easton hedged, scratching the back of his head. "That's kind of up in the air right now."

"Why?"

"There's been . . . a development."

Her courage gone, Lani quietly lowered herself down to the bottom stair. For once, Puna had been wrong, and she was glad she hadn't knocked on the door. Easton needed to

199

let his family know about her before her nose took center stage on the screen.

She probably shouldn't eavesdrop, and yet she couldn't help it.

"What sort of development?" the woman asked.

"I met someone."

A pause and then a masculine voice sounded. "You meet a lot of people during your travels."

"Her name is Lani," Easton forged on, "And she's . . . special."

Another pause and the feminine voice returned. "How old is this Lani?"

Easton chuckled. "Old enough to consider coming back to Boston with me."

More silence, and the woman's voice came again, sounding distrustful. "Are you messing with us again, son? Is Lani the name of a doll you're bringing home for Sadie? If so, it's not funny. You know I've been praying for years that you'd meet someone, and now . . . Well, have you or haven't you? Who is she, really? And I mean *really*."

"Her name is Lokelani, actually, which also happens to be the name of the island flower here on Maui. They're both beautiful, by the way. Maybe I'll bring the flower back too."

Lani had to smile at that. He'd taken the time to look up the meaning of her name. It made her heart flutter like the delicate wings of a Hawaiian Blue.

"Easton Allard, will you be serious for once in your life and tell me what's going on?"

"I am being serious," he said. "I would have introduced her to you tonight, but she wanted to watch a movie instead."

Lani had to cover her mouth to keep from laughing out loud.

"Is Lani over the age of ten?" asked his mother.

"Um . . . I think so," said Easton, "though I've never asked how old she is because that wouldn't be polite."

"Honestly, I never know when to believe him or not," his mother said, probably directing the question at his father. "For all I know, Lani is the name of a tropical fish he's bringing home for Caleb to overfeed."

Easton laughed. "Speaking of Caleb, where did he go? I'm feeling abandoned."

"And I'm feeling frustrated," muttered his mother. "Why couldn't I have gotten a son who could be straight with me? Wait . . . you are . . . *straight*, aren't you?"

"Oh please," his father grumbled. "Of course he is. Or have you already forgotten all the girls he chased in high school. I even caught him making out with a few of them."

"Actually they chased *him*," his mother said.

Easton chuckled again, and Lani frowned. Then she berated herself for eavesdropping. She should have marched up the stairs and knocked on the door to begin with.

"How's the article coming?" his father asked, no doubt trying to steer the conversation to a less frustrating place for his wife's sake. Lani could have hugged him for it.

"All done, believe it or not. I'm giving it a few days to chill on my computer, then I'll look over it one last time and send it in. But I have to say that it's good—one of the best articles I've ever written. I'm excited to see what comes of it."

"If it's really done, why aren't you on a plane right now?" asked his mother.

"I already told you, Mom. The *development*."

"Will you please stop teasing your poor mother?" said his father. "You've given her more gray hairs during the past eight years than all three of your sisters combined, and that's saying something."

"Sorry, Mom," Easton said contritely.

Still listening in, Lani leaned her head against the railing. She liked getting to know his family this way, when they could be themselves and not worry about impressing or inspecting The Development.

"A few weeks ago, you were still stressing about that article. What did you finally decide to write about?" his father asked.

"A place the locals call Kapu Aina. You have to jump off three waterfalls to get there, but it's incredible. A natural hot springs, cascading falls, and an off-the-beaten-path swimming hole surrounded by a paradisiacal jungle. The cherry on top? It's never been written about before, at least not that I can find."

Lani slowly lifted her head as a cold chill ran down her back. Kapu Aina? His article was about *her* Kapu Aina? *Ahe's* Kapu Aina? *Her friends'* Kapu Aina?

Please no.

"I'm telling you, when *National Geographic* runs the article, the exposure I'll get will be epic. And if my page views increase by the amount that I'm thinking they could, I'll be able to double my advertising fees."

National Geographic? He was a writer for *National Geographic?* He was a travel *reporter?* Lani gripped the post as the pounding in her heart reverberated in her head. Voices faded to the background as thoughts, questions, and accusations thudded through her mind.

What had he written in that article? Had he documented how to get there? Taken pictures? No, he couldn't have. It had been too dark and she would have noticed.

And then it hit her. The week after the hike, he hadn't gone MIA because he'd been avoiding her. He'd been doing his homework. He'd probably gone back to the place they'd parked and retraced their steps, taken a myriad of pictures, and hand-picked the best ones to go with his article, along with directions on where to park, possibly even a map. Would her once-sacred Kapu Aina soon become a popular tourist destination?

Her stomach lurched, and Lani leaned forward, feeling like she might heave at any moment. It was because of her that Ahe had invited Easton. All because of her.

She'd unwittingly let Easton use her. No wonder he'd been so secretive about his work, why he'd wanted an invite to Ahe's potluck, to all the parties and get-togethers, the surfing, fishing . . . Kapu Aina. All this time, Lani had flattered herself into thinking it was because he was interested in her, when in reality, he'd wanted an "in" to the local's hot spots.

How could she have been so blind? How could she have fallen so hard for someone who . . .

A searing pain registered in her forehead, and Lani pressed her fist against it, hoping for some relief. None of this made any sense. She and Easton had talked of building a future together. They'd made plans. He'd told her he loved her and had just told his parents about her. Was any of that true?

Yes.

Lani had seen the truth of it in his eyes, felt it in his touch. His article was already written, and yet he was still here, planning a future with her—the woman he was about to betray. *How could he?* He knew how much Kapu Aina meant to her, to Ahe's family, to her friends. How could he possibly be okay with sharing that with the rest of the world?

Apparently Easton Allard wasn't the man she thought he was. If he really cared about her—about anyone—he wouldn't even think of doing this to her and the people she loved. Based on his relationship with his family, Lani thought he understood the meaning of love, loyalty, and friendship, but he couldn't, not really—not if he was willing to barter it all for money and recognition and whatever else he hoped to achieve.

Maybe the only person Easton really cared about was himself.

The pain struck deep inside Lani's soul, attacking and destroying, crushing and breaking, molding her heart into a lifeless crater.

Words from Tennyson echoed in her ears. *'Tis better to have loved and lost than never to have loved at all.*

What a lie.

From inside the bungalow, Easton laughed, and more voices joined the conversation. Lani couldn't listen any longer. She pulled herself up and stumbled down the hill, furious at Easton for what he'd done and was about to do.

At the bottom, Pearl stood just outside the door, smelling the orchids. She looked up to see Lani rush past, but she didn't ask questions or say anything. She let Lani run inside and hide behind the closed door of her bedroom.

Thirty minutes later, a knock sounded.

"Lani," said her grandmother. "Easton's here to see you. Everything okay?"

Lani swallowed the lump in her throat and continued to stare at her bedroom ceiling, forcing her words to remain even as she answered. "I think I'm coming down with something. Would you tell him I'll talk to him tomorrow?"

"Oh no, I'm so sorry to hear that. Can I get you anything?"

"I just need some sleep."

"If you're sure."

"Yes."

A pause and then her footsteps padded away. Murmuring voices sounded, a door closed, and her grandmother's footsteps returned, pausing for a few moments outside her door before moving on.

Lani sighed in relief. She couldn't talk to anyone right now—not even Puna. Every part of her body throbbed from a pain that came from deep inside. She stared at the ceiling until the light coming through the cracks in her door flickered off and silence reigned. Around one o'clock, she wiped away the last of her tears and curled into a ball on her side, but it wasn't until sometime between three and four that she finally fell asleep.

When the morning light crept in her bedroom window and woke her up, she dragged herself to the shower, hoping that would help. When it didn't, she found her way to the office, desperate for a distraction.

The first email she opened was a cancellation for the Akua room for that afternoon. An hour later, when Pearl breezed in, looking as beautiful and put-together as always, and announced she'd decided to stay for a day or two longer, Lani wasn't surprised at all.

"I'm glad you're staying, Pearl. I really am," Lani said. "But if the reason you're staying is why I think it is, there's really no point."

"I don't know what you're talking about. I'm staying because I'm hoping to see the Orange Frost Banksia bloom before I go."

Lani didn't have it in her to inform Pearl that the flower wouldn't be in bloom for another month or two at least. Instead, she clicked Delete on the cancellation and said, "For you, I'm sure it will."

chapter 20

L ani was in the kitchen, baking, when Easton walked in
   and closed the door, folding his arms across his chest.
   Lani hated that her heart constricted, mourned, and
crumbled all over again.

"You're avoiding me again."

Lani finished pouring the batter into the bread pan,
then slid the three loaves into the oven. "I don't feel good,
that's all."

He moved toward her, arms still folded. "Sick people
stay in bed. They don't get up at the crack of dawn, lock
themselves in their office for hours, then bake"—he glanced
around at all the loaves of banana bread lined up in neat
rows across the counter and island—"five dozen loaves of
bread."

"There's only three dozen," Lani corrected.

He closed the distance between them and placed his
hands on her shoulders, which she quickly shrugged off.
Then she walked to the other side of the island, keeping it
between them.

"What's going on?" he asked, taking a few steps back. "Yesterday afternoon we were talking about you coming home to meet my family and now you won't even let me touch you. And don't give me some lame excuse about not feeling well. The truth, *please*."

The demand was enough to ignite Lani's ire. "You want the truth?"

"Yes."

"Yeah, well good. Because so do I."

Crinkle lines appeared on his forehead. "Am I missing something?"

"No. But you made sure I did. Otherwise you would have told me you were working on an article for *National Geographic* and decided to make it about Kapu Aina. I heard everything last night. If you wanted to keep that conversation private, you should have closed your windows."

Lani had expected a reaction of surprise, guilt, possibly even remorse. Instead he blinked at her then lifted his palms in a gesture that said, *And the problem is . . . ?*

"Are you mad I didn't tell you?" he finally asked.

"Yes . . . I mean no . . . I mean—yes! I'm mad that you weren't honest with me from the get-go, but mostly I'm upset that you wrote about Kapu Aina. It's a special place to all of us here because it's one of the few remaining spots that hasn't been tarnished by tourism. We trusted you enough to show it to you, and now you're about to betray that trust and take Kapu Aina away from us—from me. *How could you?*" Tears threatened to come yet again, making Lani more angry. She'd cried enough over this already.

Easton held up a hand as though trying to calm her down. "Lani, Kapu Aina isn't yours. It isn't Ahe's. It isn't anyone else's. It's on public land."

"The only way out is through *private* land—through a

friend's property who allows *us* to use it, not a bunch of tourists."

"The shortest and easiest way out is through private land. But if you continue to follow the river down for another mile or so, then head directly south for another mile, you can stay on public land."

Lani's entire body trembled. She had never wanted to punch someone as much as she wanted to punch him in that moment. "What did you do, go back and map it all out? Take a bunch of pictures so people can find their way without getting lost?"

"That's exactly what I did."

Her fingers tightened into fists and her jaw clenched. "And you didn't have a problem doing that? No twinge of conscience? No guilt? No thought about how wrong it is?"

Easton planted his palms on the island and met her gaze directly. "Lani, tourism isn't an annoyance that only exists on Maui. Any beautiful, unique, or rare find that is shared with the world becomes a destination for people who want to see it as well. The Grand Canyon, the Aogashima Volcano, Glow Worm Cave, Ha Long Bay, Giant's Causeway—the list goes on and on. Even my favorite little hike back in Boston was posted about on Facebook, Instagrammed, and linked on Pinterest. It's been years since I could hike that trail without running into a bunch of families or trail-runners or pet-owners taking their dog out for a jaunt. It's called *sharing*."

Lani jabbed a finger at him. "Don't you dare make me the bad guy here. You knew exactly what you were doing the moment you decided to come here. That's why you were so secretive and mysterious—because you also knew that if I, or any of the locals, found out you travel writer, you would have never gotten more than an aloha from any of us."

"I told you that I wrote about my experiences."

"Yeah, in such a vague way that I was led to believe that you wrote about cultures, about people, about the aloha spirit and life in Hawaii. You never once told me you worked for *National Geographic*."

"I don't. I'm only writing one article for them, and only because I won their traveler of the year award. The prize was an all-expenses paid trip to anywhere in the world, along with a two-page spread in their magazine."

Lani pounded her palm into the counter. "Why did you have to choose Maui? *Why?*"

"I didn't," he said. "I would never have chosen Maui—not in a million years. But I made the mistake of letting my readers decide for me, thinking it would drive up my page views if I got them involved, which it did, so here I am."

"All I heard was that you care more about your bottom line than people."

"Of course I care about my bottom line," he said, his voice rising. "And I'm willing to bet that you do too. We have to care. It's called survival and self-reliance and finding a way to support whatever lifestyle we choose for ourselves. Do you know why I got chosen as traveler of the year? Because I had the courage to walk away from a normal life and make traveling a career. I started off as an international house-sitter to save on accommodations. I picked up odd jobs anywhere I could get them, whether it was shoveling manure and feeding animals or donning a conical hat and picking rice in the fields of Cambodia. During the hours I didn't work, I met people, I explored cities, towns, country sides, oceans, and wrote about my experiences.

"I started a blog and began journaling everything, posting pictures of places not yet published on the internet, and as I did, I started to gain a following. Gradually, my readership grew big enough so companies are now willing to pay me to advertise on my site. I also make a little through affiliate links, through connecting people to house-sitting opportunities, and I've published a few ebooks. But all of that added together still barely pays the bills. So now I'm flirting with the idea of starting a sort of side business—a social media consulting firm to teach others what I've learned over the past several years. Because it's not about just me anymore. It's about you, too. Which is also why this *National Geographic* article is so important. It will open so many doors for me—for us—doors that need to open if we're going to make this work. So yeah, I care about the bottom line, but not more than people, and definitely not more than you."

I don't believe you, Lani wanted to shout. *Actions speak louder than words.* She felt like she'd just taken off the mask of a hero to find a villain underneath. "I feel like all this time you've pretended to be something you're not, and that's who I fell in love with—the pretend version of you."

He lifted his palms then slapped them down again for emphasis. "Give me a break. You know exactly who I am. Yes, I was evasive about what I did for a living because I know the people here are fiercely protective of what few secrets they have left, and I understand why they are. I, too, was annoyed when someone first posted about my favorite hike. But once I got over that, instead of hearing noise and seeing crowds and footprints and people getting in my way, I saw smiling faces of kids looking at something besides a TV or computer screen. I saw parents shoving their phone into their pockets and interacting with their kids, couples holding hands, and pets being taken for walks. I saw joy and peace and a greater appreciation for nature. I saw *life*."

Tears pooled in Lani's eyes. She shook her head, feeling like he was refusing to understand something that he should know better than anyone else. "The people of Hawaii are the most kind and giving people I have ever met. They'd give you the shirt off their back if they thought you needed it. So don't make this about selfishness because it's not about that, and you know it. It's about preserving a place that is special to them and special to me. When Kapu Aina is quiet and calm, you feel a connection to the land that you could never feel with people swarming and talking and laughing around you. Maui has given tourists the Pipiwai trail, the pools at Ohe'o, Hamoa, and the black and red sand beaches, and countless other places. They don't need Kapu Aina too. But we do." Lani's resolve broke and tears fell freely from her eyes. "Why can't you understand that?"

The silence squeezed in around her, pushing against her body and thudding in her head. Every inch of Lani ached. Her head, her body, her spirit—but mostly, her heart. It felt shredded and misshapen and worn, as though Easton had taken it in his fist and crumpled the life out of it.

"I don't want to lose you over this," he finally said, his voice sounding like background noise to all the thrumming in her head.

Lani closed her eyes, unable to look at him any longer. "Your article is finished," she said. "I think it's time for you to leave."

"You can't mean that." She heard him move and felt his presence at her side, but he didn't try to touch her.

She gripped the counter harder and squeezed her eyes tighter closed. *Go away. Please, just go away,* she chanted over and over in her mind.

Finally, he did. His presence faded away, the door opened and closed, and the smell of burning banana bread filled her senses.

Lani quickly shut off the oven, yanked open the door, and tossed the ruined bread *and* the pans into the garbage can, then bolted out the back door. Right now, she needed Kapu Aina more than ever—and she'd escape there before it became overrun with visitors.

Easton returned from a lengthy, emotionally-purging run and grabbed a sports drink from the mini-fridge in the bungalow. He guzzled it, then looked out the window to the beautiful scenery beyond, feeling a strange sense of claustrophobia.

His gaze landed on his laptop, and he sighed. Even though he'd presented his case like any good lawyer would have done, he'd also withheld a few things—like how he'd wrestled with his decision to write about Kapu Aina, how he'd battled to contain the torrent of words that flowed from his mind about it, and how he'd rationalized that inspiration like that wouldn't have come if it was wrong to publish it.

He'd told his parents it needed one more revision, but it didn't. Every word was exactly where it needed to be. Easton could have emailed it to the editor days ago, if not for the one thing that had held him back.

Lani.

When she'd finally confronted him about it, Easton had almost been relieved. He'd been trying to figure out a way to tell her all weekend, but the right moment never happened. So he was glad to finally get it out in the open—to tell his side and hope she'd see things the way he did. Unfortunately, it had all backfired, and now he was left with a decision to make. Actually, it wasn't a decision at all.

His feet dragging, Easton treaded across the room and picked up his laptop. He sat down, lifted the screen from the keyboard, and read through the article one last time before exiting out of it. Then he clicked New Document, and a blank page appeared. He stared at it for five full minutes before he began writing.

This time, the words didn't flow at all. Easton had to pry them from his brain like an unripe berry from a plant. That's how they read too—unripe, broken, and all wrong.

But he forged on. Minutes and hours ticked by as he pried, deleted, and yanked some more. Then he revised and revised and revised. By nightfall, he finally had the bones of something that could be decent. His stomach growled, and Easton glanced at the clock in the bottom corner of his laptop—11:17. He thought of all the loaves of banana bread Lani had baked that morning and wondered if she and Cora had already given them away or if they'd mind if he helped himself to one. After this morning, Lani might, but Cora probably wouldn't.

He shut his laptop and wandered outside, breathing in the lush, tropical scent that had so often cleansed his mind. When no mind-cleansing came, he sighed. Still, it still felt better to be outside than inside. He trotted down the steps, noting that all the lights were off in the main house. Would the door be open? The kitchen window?

"You're up late." Pearl's voice came out of nowhere, making Easton flinch. He looked over and saw her sitting in the shadows on the main lanai.

"So are you," he said, walking over to her.

Her hands were clutched loosely together on her lap. "I was waiting for you, actually. I thought you might get hungry for something more than a granola bar."

A smile lifted his mouth, and it felt good. "You know me too well, I guess. I was just contemplating how I could break into the kitchen and sneak a loaf of bread."

"You're in luck." Pearl reached over and picked up a loaf that had been sitting on the seat next to her. It was wrapped in plastic and looked so good that Easton's stomach rumbled again.

She held it out to him. "Cora brought me three of these this afternoon. She said Lani had spent the morning trying to rid the island of bananas. I think she tried to stop by the bungalow too, but no one answered."

"Mahalo," he said, accepting the bread. "I haven't eaten since breakfast. I've been . . . busy."

"I could tell," she said. "Will you be leaving soon also?"

"Yeah." He nodded. "I'm thinking tomorrow, actually, assuming there's a seat available. You headed out as well?"

"Soon," she said. "There are a few things that need to be straightened out first."

He had the strangest idea she was referring to him and Lani, but that was ridiculous and Easton wasn't about to ask for clarification. He looked around and drew in a deep breath.

"I'm going to miss this place."

Pearl nodded in her understanding way. "I will too. But for me, it will become a fond memory—a part of my past. For you, it could become so much more. It could become part of your future."

Easton tucked the bread under one arm and shoved his hands into his pockets. "I'm not so sure about that, Pearl. I messed up."

She rested her hands on the armrests, then leaned forward and pushed herself up. She took two steps toward him before clasping her fingers together again. "People mess up. It's what we do, what we're good at. But that doesn't mean it can't be fixed."

He nodded, knowing the truth of her words, but not feeling them. "I'm trying to fix it, but . . . if you'd only seen the look on Lani's face earlier, well . . . you'd have your doubts too."

Pearl smiled sympathetically. "I've seen lots of pain in my life, but I've also seen a lot of joy, and when joy blossoms from pain, it's more exquisite. Don't look down on yourself for too long, Easton. It is so much better to look up."

Easton studied Pearl for a moment, wondering about her history, about what she'd been through, about how she'd become so wise and good and kind. She had never asked what he'd done wrong. Maybe she already knew or maybe she didn't. It didn't seem to matter. In her eyes, all downs could become ups if a person wanted it badly enough.

"Mahalo, Pearl. For that"—he held up the loaf of bread—"and this. I'm glad you waited up for me."

She dipped her head in acknowledgement. "Good night, Easton." Then she walked down the steps, lifted her face to the stars, and sauntered back to her room.

Easton took her advice and looked up on his way back to the bungalow. Thousands of stars glittered in a rich, black sky. It wasn't the first time he'd looked up at night. He'd done it often in his travels and could point out several constellations—both in the northern hemisphere and the southern. But tonight they looked different to him. Brighter maybe, like they'd been recharged. The feeling seemed to surge down and envelop him, giving him a renewed sense of energy and purpose.

Mahalo, Pearl, he thought as he jogged up the bungalow's steps.

Once inside, he ate a thick slice of bread before picking up his laptop again. He highlighted all the words he'd spent half the day writing and deleted them. With a white, blank page staring back at him, Easton began anew.

chapter 21

Lani drove to Kahului in the morning. She made sure the fridge was stocked with enough food to feed the guests, then left a note for Puna and headed out. Kapu Aina had been as beautiful and peaceful as always, but everywhere she looked she saw Easton, felt Easton, thought about Easton. She needed to get away from Hāna, to a place that would be free of him, and she might as well pick up some supplies while she was at it.

Since Costco wasn't yet open, she stopped at Kanaha Beach and let the breeze whip her hair as she watched the windsurfers glide across the water. It probably felt so freeing to fly over the ocean like that. Maybe she should give it a try. It might be a close enough second to soaring.

As the hour neared ten, she brushed the sand from her shorts and drove to the store. She wandered down every aisle, taking her time, and two hours later, she left with a tank full of gas, a truck filled with food and supplies, and a more positive state of mind. She finally felt ready to face Easton again without crumbling.

As she rounded one of the bends on the highway, she could have sworn she saw Easton pass her in his rented black Subaru. But before she could decipher the plates in her rearview mirror, the car disappeared. No, it couldn't have been him. He would never leave without saying goodbye. He'd promised.

The rest of the way back, Lani's stomach felt squeamish. And when Puna informed her that Easton had checked out an hour before, squeamish became nauseous. Just like that, he was gone.

You told him to leave, remember? came an annoying voice of reason.

And yet Lani had held onto the hope that until he said goodbye, it wasn't really over. But he'd broken his promise like he'd broken her trust, heart, and everything else. She shouldn't be surprised or devastated or anything but grateful.

But she was devastated.

"He left a note on your desk in the office," Puna said, her voice sympathetic. Then she gave Lani's arm a squeeze and began unloading the supplies. Her grandmother seemed to understand that Lani would talk when she was ready, and until that time, Puna would wait.

After they'd unloaded the groceries, Lani glanced at the bungalow, knowing she would need to eventually ready it for whatever purpose Puna wanted it to serve after Easton, but she didn't know if she'd ever be able to walk inside it again. No wonder her grandmother had left the place untouched for so long. Painful memories acted like a force field, keeping people away.

By late afternoon, Lani couldn't avoid the office any

longer. She needed to answer some emails and send out a packet of brochures, so she squared her shoulders and walked inside. She found Pearl there, waiting with her suitcases.

No. Not Pearl too!

"I think I've stayed long enough," said Pearl with a kind smile. "It's time for me to move on."

You can't leave yet! Lani wanted to shout. *I need your wisdom now more than ever. I'm not ready for you to go.*

That expectation was unfair and selfish, and Lani immediately felt contrite. "I know I've told you this already, but I'm going to miss you."

"Goodbyes are always difficult, especially between good friends," said Pearl, clasping Lani's hands between hers. "But don't worry. Life will go on and things will look up in time. That, I promise."

"I hope you're right." But Pearl's leaving felt so final, like it really was over. And if it really was over, then . . .

"I see someone left a note here for you," said Pearl, pointing to an envelope with Lani's name scribbled across the front in masculine ALL CAPS. A silver key sat on top, attached to a key chain with the inscription: "The Bungalow."

Lani tried to swallow the lump lodged in her throat, but it wouldn't budge. "Looks like it."

"Someone once told me that to love a person is to see them for who they really are, then remind them of it when they've forgotten. I've always thought that was very good advice."

Before Lani could reply, Pearl pulled her into a quick hug and said, "Goodbye, my dear." Then she picked up her bags, smiled one last time, and walked out the door. Lani waited for the jingle, but it didn't come. Pearl had left the way she'd come.

As the silence enveloped her, Lani's gaze was drawn to the desk where Easton's note seemed to call out to her, willing her to open it. Her fingers twitched until she snatched up the envelope and tore into it. Inside, she found a handwritten note and a typewritten article.

She read the note first.

> *Lokelani,*
>
> *By the time you get this, I'll be on my way back to Boston. You're probably thinking I broke my promise and left without saying goodbye, but this isn't a goodbye. It's more of a full disclosure.*
>
> *You're right that I've kept a part of myself hidden from you, and I was wrong to do that. I want you to see the real me—the whole me—and decide for yourself who I really am. Attached is the article I've already sent to* National Geographic. *I hope you read it, and I hope you read some of my blog as well.*
>
> *I don't want to close the door on you, so I'm leaving it wide open with the hope that you'll choose to walk through it one day and give us a second chance.*
>
> *I will always love you.*
>
> *Easton*
>
> *(TravelingEast.com)*
>
> *P.S. My middle name is Gordon, named after my grandpa.*

Lani's fingers shook as she put down the note and picked up the printout.

Rachael Anderson

Looking Up
by Easton Gordon

I was on the island of São Miguel in the Azores when I first heard I'd been chosen as the recipient for National Geographic's Traveler of the Year *Award. I immediately hiked Pico da Vara, the highest point on the island, and at an elevation of only 3,916 feet, I felt like I was on top of the world and nothing could get me down.*

And then I did something many people do when they're high. I did something stupid. I hosted a contest on my blog and let my readers decide my next destination (which also happened to be the subject for this article). When Maui rose to the top of the survey, I wanted nothing more than to take back my right to choose and pick somewhere else.

Let me explain. Book after book, article after article has already been written about Maui. It's been done, over and over and over again. How was I, in only three months' time, supposed to deliver what my blog, TravelingEast, has always promised: A unique experience that most people have never read about before. I knew in my soul I couldn't.

So it was with major trepidation that I flew to Maui. I spent two days in Kihei, two more in Lahaina, and another in Kaanapali. Everywhere I drove, hiked, and searched was a picture I'd already seen multiple times somewhere else. I couldn't compete. So I threw a Hail Mary and headed to Hāna, knowing I was putting all of my eggs in a very small basket. 11.7 square miles to be exact. Population 1,235.

It was there I found exactly what I was searching for, though I didn't know it at the time.

A wise woman once told me that it's better to look up than down. I used to think I was pretty good at doing that, but in Hāna I was taught to look a little higher—or deeper, I guess you could say.

And when I did, my perspective changed. I saw a rare, Hawaiian Blue butterfly, touched the leaves of a sensitive plant, tasted the world's most incredible banana bread, learned how to sense the ocean and anticipate a wave, and fell in love with a rose named Lokelani, which happens to be the island flower of Maui. Lani means heavenly in Hawaiian, and it's the perfect description. The flower is beautiful and soft, wild and lively, and smells like sunshine. Someday, I hope to explain on my blog why I'm so fascinated with that flower, but for now that secret stays with me.

I used to think that all Maui had to offer was the commonly known beauties like Haleakalā, the Seven Sacred Pools, and Kaanapali Beach. It wasn't until I'd spent the majority of the summer in Hāna that I realized the discoveries here are endless. If you come in search of an adventure, you'll find it. If you come to learn something new, you will. If you're looking for a break from the grind of daily living, welcome to Maui, a place that offers you, me—everyone—the chance to take home something that will be uniquely yours and yours alone. Maybe it will be the burning image of a spectacular sunset, the awe of experiencing a Brocken spectre, or the sensation of a sea turtle's flippers tickling your back as it swims past. Whatever it is, you can't come to Maui and not look up.

Ever so slowly, Lani set down the article. She ignored the invoices, the reservations waiting to be confirmed, the brochures needing to be stuffed and mailed, and the message light blinking on the phone. She pulled up the internet, typed in "TravelingEast.com," and waited what felt like an eternity for it to load. A beautiful and professional website appeared with Easton's picture at the top. His handsome face smiled at her, making her heart lurch and hope and even heal a bit.

Then she began reading. She learned that Easton's "pen name" was Easton Gordon. She learned that he enjoyed getting to know the locals. He'd run races, attended celebrations, helped rebuild a church in Taiwan that had burned down, and even coached a soccer team in Peru. He seemed to love every place he'd visited, from congested cities to primitive towns, but he was definitely a fan of the great outdoors.

As the hours rolled by, Lani was reminded of what had drawn her to Easton in the first place—his sense of humor, his laid-back personality, his charm and charisma. If she'd stumbled across his blog before she knew him, she would have been sucked in just like the rest of his readers. He had a gift for storytelling and viewing the world with acceptance and respect.

As evening approached, Lani had reached Easton's third year of traveling. Even though her eyes were bleary and her stomach rumbling, Lani still couldn't turn away. It read like a novel that she couldn't put down until the end. Only with the blog, she was reading to find out how it all began.

That's when Puna found her.

"Ah, here you are," she said. "I've been looking everywhere for you. What's that you're reading?"

"Easton's travel blog," said Lani, sounding more like a robot than human. Her emotions were all over the place. If she poured them into a large bowl and mixed them all together to balance them out, the end result might not feel like anything.

Eyes still on the computer screen, Lani said, "He wrote about Kapu Aina, you know—with details, pictures, directions, everything. He got to know us so he could discover our secrets, then he was planning to publish it in a national magazine and tell the world."

Lani twisted in her seat and looked at her grandmother—really looked at her. What would Puna think of Easton now? More than anything, Lani wanted to do as Pearl suggested and see past this, but every time she thought of how he'd used her and her friends and what he could have done, a throb began in her gut and spread through her body. Trust was key to any relationship. Without it . . .

Puna dragged over a chair and sat down. She took her granddaughter's hand in hers and gave it a squeeze. "That's the first time I've heard you refer to yourself as one of the locals."

Lani rubbed her bleary eyes with her free hand. "*That's* what you got out of my comment? Didn't you hear the part about Easton writing about Kapu Aina?"

"I also heard you say the word 'was.' I take it he's changed his mind about publishing the article?"

"Well, yes, but that's not the point."

"It's exactly the point." Puna patted Lani's hand. "He listened, he reevaluated, and he changed his mind because he cares about you, *mea aloha*. People make mistakes. It's how they go about fixing them that matters."

Lani drew her lower lip into her mouth and nodded. "Did you and Kuku Kane ever argue?"

"Heavens, yes," said her grandmother with a laugh. "Early on in our marriage, every so often he would disappear into the mountains without telling me where he was going or when he'd be back. Sometimes he was gone for hours. Others, overnight. He called it soul-searching. Then one day, he left and didn't return for two days. Two days! I was certain he'd been bitten by a poisonous spider or fell off a cliff or something horrible. I called everyone I knew and was busy organizing a search when he'd finally searched his soul enough to wander back home. I was madder than an angry bee and told him that if he ever did that to me again, he'd come home to an empty house. From that point on, he never left without telling me, and he was never gone for more than twenty-four hours again."

Lani smiled at the story.

How much had changed in so short a time. Like a strong riptide in the ocean, the summer had swept her up and carried her to a place far from where she'd started. Although it felt unchartered and scary, as she looked below the surface, Lani could see a world brimming with life, hope, and possibilities. All she had to do was take a deep breath and dive.

Lani smoothed her palms along the fabric of her shorts, feeling a nervous energy that made her fidgety. "Puna, if I get everything organized and make sure we have enough supplies on hand, how would you feel about holding down the fort for a few days?"

Her grandmother's eyes crinkled at the corners, as did her mouth. "I'd say things are already organized, and we have more than enough supplies, thanks to your frequent runs to Costco. Perhaps tomorrow would be a great time to show Maaike around and teach her a thing or two about the business."

Trembling now, Lani wrapped her grandmother into a hug. "I'll be back," she whispered.

"Only you?" Puna asked.

"I meant *we'll* be back. I hope."

"Of course you will," said Puna, as though it had never occurred to her that Lani wouldn't. "You said it yourself. You're a local now and this is your home. But don't feel like you have to rush back anytime soon either. Believe it or not, I know how to pay bills, confirm reservations, make breakfast, and clean rooms. I was doing it long before you got here."

"I know," said Lani, knowing her grandmother wasn't as young or spry as she used to be. "But it's a lot of work for one person."

"Especially one as old as I am is what you're thinking."

"I'd never."

Puna smiled. "It is a lot of work, but with Maaike's help, I can manage. Now book your flight, go to Boston, and put that poor boy out of his misery."

chapter 22

"King me!" Easton told his seven-year-old nephew after his black checker's piece had hopped over Skyler's red one and landed on the last row.

"Ah, man!" A mop of straight, blond hair fell forward over Skyler's forehead as he whined. He glared as he slammed another black checker on top of Easton's. "You always win."

"I haven't won yet. But if that's the attitude you're going to adopt, I'm sure I will. Where's your sanguinity, dude?"

"My *what*?" Skyler looked at Easton as though he'd just stepped out of a time machine. His blue eyes sizzled in frustration, and his pale, round face had a pinkish hue to it.

Easton held back a smile. "It means cheerfully optimistic."

"Optim-what?" Skyler's fuse looked ready to blow.

Easton knew that goading his nephew was a risky move. Skyler's personality was nothing if not volatile, but it was also predictable. He'd either overturn the checkerboard and stomp away, or he'd do as Easton hoped—get some tenacity.

"I thought you were in school," Easton said, pushing him further. "Don't you listen to your vocabulary lessons?"

"Yes," Skyler growled. "Last week we learned about armadillions and lumbering and troublemakers."

"It's armadill*os*, not amadill*ions*. And you already know what a troublemaker is. You see one every day in the mirror."

Skylers chubby fingers became fists and his cheeks reddened. But the checkerboard was still upright, which was a good sign. "I'm *not* a troublemaker."

"You're right. You're just a quitter."

"No. I'm. *Not*."

"Prove it." Easton nodded toward the board. "Show me you can win this game."

Face still red, Skyler's expression became one of complete concentration as he redirected his frustration to the board. He stared, he studied, and he kept his finger on pieces as he experimented with different moves. Finally, after what felt like hours, he pushed a red piece forward in a move that actually impressed Easton.

It impressed him so much that for the first time since he'd introduced Skyler to the game three years earlier, he allowed his nephew beat him.

Skyler's hands shot in the air, and his body followed. "Yes!" he shouted. "I am the new Checkers king! No one can stop me now!"

Easton chuckled and mussed the top of Skyler's head. "Let this be a lesson to you. Never, ever, *ever* give up. If you put your mind to something, anything is possible."

But Skyler didn't care about the lesson. He only cared that he was the new king of Checkers, and he couldn't wait to gloat to his little brother, Caleb, and share the news with Grandpa—both of whom were trimming the bushes out back.

"You're going to make a great father one day," commented his mother from the kitchen. She slid a homemade pizza into the oven and brushed her hands together to rid them of the flour.

She'd meant it as a compliment, but it only served to remind Easton that it had been six days since he'd seen Lani, and he hadn't gotten so much as a text from her. Had she seen his note? Read his article? Or had she pitched them without opening the envelope?

Maybe he needed to take his own advice and not give up. Why had he left Maui anyway? Why hadn't he stayed and groveled his way back into her life like he'd groveled for so many invites?

Because when it came to this, he couldn't. Like with Checkers, it was Lani's move, and no matter how much he wanted to push her piece in his direction, he couldn't do it for her.

Lani's body quivered as she stood on the front porch, waiting for someone to answer. The home was larger than she'd expected, much grander than Puna's thirteen-hundred-square-foot home. Built with beautiful red bricks, white columns flanked the entry and black shutters snuggled against each white-paned window. Her fingers played with the folds of her knee-length, turquoise dress, and her feet felt trapped in beaded flip-flops. It had been a long journey to get here, and she had no idea what to expect when that door opened. What if Easton wasn't home? What if he'd told his family about the girl who'd been so quick to judge and send him away, and she was about to meet his family alone? What would she do? Ask to stay and wait? Or call another cab to take her . . . where, she wasn't sure.

Maybe she should have sent a text to let Easton know she was coming.

A petite woman opened the door. She wasn't slender or large either. Just . . . perfect. Shoulder-length, straight brown hair, skin that had begun to wrinkle, and green eyes that looked so much like Easton's Lani nearly lost her train of thought.

"Hello," said the woman Lani assumed was Easton's mother. "May I help you?"

Lani cleared her throat, hoping her voice wouldn't squeak. "Yes, actually. I'm, uh . . . looking for Easton Allard?"

"Oh," said the woman. "Well, you've come to the right place. Come on in, and I'll—oh, there you are."

Standing behind his mother, Easton's eyes glinted at Lani from under the brim of a black and red Boston Red Sox cap. Her heart came alive. It had only been about a week since she'd last seen him, but it felt like months—long enough for her to worry about how he'd react to seeing her on his doorstep.

His mom took a few steps to the side, opening a path between them.

Lani drew in a deep breath, trying to look more confident than she felt. "Hi. I'm here to . . . um . . . walk through the door. If it's still open." She could only imagine how odd that must sound to his mother, who probably had no idea who she was.

Since Easton still hadn't made a peep, Lani turned to the woman and held out her hand. "You must be Easton's mother. I'm a friend of his from Hawaii. My name is Lani Whitman."

His mother's eyes widened in surprise. She even mouthed Lani's name before blitzing forward and flinging her arms around the stranger standing on her front porch. When she pulled back there were even tears in her eyes.

She grasped Lani by the shoulders. "Oh my goodness, you really do exist! I had my hopes, but when Easton showed up with a tropical fish in a bag that he'd named Lani, I couldn't figure out if he was teasing me or—but now you're here, a real live person, and so beautiful too, and oh my goodness, I don't know what to say. Why don't you come in? We're just about to have dinner."

Her arm moved from Lani's shoulder to her waist, and Lani felt herself being guided inside—at least until Easton intervened with a hand on his mother's arm.

"Mom," he said quietly, then jerked his head toward the kitchen.

"Oh. Of course." His mother's hands dropped to her side, and she took a few steps toward the kitchen before pausing and looking back. Her shoulders relaxed, and her voice became calm and gracious. "There's plenty of pizza, Lani, if you'd like to stay for dinner. Tonight, it's just me and my husband and my two grandsons. And Easton, of course."

Lani smiled, loving the warmth and kindness his mother exuded. "I'd love to, Mrs. Allard. Thank you."

"Please, call me Gail." She practically floated away, leaving Lani alone with Easton.

He took her gently by the arm and pulled her onto the front porch, closing the door behind them. A car drove past, a woman was out walking her dog, and across the street a neighbor mowed his lawn. But Lani didn't care. Easton was staring at her in a way that made her forget to breathe.

"You're here," he said.

"Yes."

"To stay."

"For a few days, at least."

He let out a breath and grinned. "What changed your mind?"

"You. And Pearl. And Puna. But mostly you. I loved your article."

"Yeah?"

"And your blog."

A twinkle appeared in his eyes. "And . . .?"

The question reminded her of all the times he'd hinted for invites in his endearing, not-so-subtle ways.

"You," she whispered.

His smile stretched wide, and his laugh was more breath than sound. "I'm grinning like a fool, aren't I?"

"It looks good on you."

He moved in close, and his palms cupped the side of her face. His eyes held warmth and tenderness.

"I love you, too," he said. And then he kissed her. His hands threaded through her hair while his lips moved across hers. Lani melted against him, feeling invigorated and weak at the same time. She clung to him, loving the way his touch made her skin tingle, the peppermint on his breath, and the lingering scent of his aftershave. Lani used to think that surfing was the only place she could ever become completely lost to a moment, but that was before she'd met Easton, before she'd felt his kiss, before she knew what it felt like to soar.

When her knees felt ready to give way, Lani's hands moved from his back to his shoulders and down his arms to his hands, where they stayed as she drew away.

"Before I let you kiss me again," she said, out of breath. "We need to talk."

"That sounds serious."

"It is," she said. "Very serious. I've just spent over nineteen hours on a plane or in airports. My luggage has been lost somewhere between here and Kahului, two of my three flights were delayed, I haven't slept hardly at all, and other than two pathetically small packages of peanuts and drinks, I haven't had anything to eat since my last layover in LA over seven hours ago."

"In other words, I should be grateful you haven't turned into Scrooge yet."

She nodded. "There is that. But, more importantly, I need to know something. Is that normal? I mean, if I really commit to traveling the world with you, is this how it's going to be a lot of the time?"

He laughed and pulled her into a bear hug, holding her close and keeping her upright. He smelled so clean that it made her more aware of how she probably smelled.

"Honestly," he said. "You have to expect some delays and lost luggage, but once you walk off that plane into a fascinating new place, somehow it doesn't matter anymore— at least not once you shower, change, and get some rest." He combed his fingers through her hair. "We can start off slow and only do as much as you're comfortable with, okay?"

"Okay," she murmured into his neck, snuggling closer as the nineteen-hour journey finally took its toll. She would fall asleep any second now.

"How is it you look so amazing after all that?" he said.

"I don't feel amazing," came her muffled reply. "But I was smart enough to carry a change of clothes in my carryon, and I freshened up in the bathroom at the Boston airport. But I would give anything for a shower right now. And there must be a window open somewhere, because that pizza smells incredible."

Easton chuckled and dropped a kiss on the top of her

head. "Let's get you a few slices, find you a shower and some comfortable clothes, and put you to bed. How does that sound?"

"Heavenly."

He kissed her again, wrapped an arm around her shoulders, and led her inside, where Lani was welcomed again, stuffed with the yummiest pizza she'd ever eaten, charmed by two adorable little boys, then turned over to the capable and loving hands of Easton's mother, who found her some clothes, a toothbrush, and showed her to the guest room and bath. As Lani lay in bed, all cozy and warm, she couldn't help but dream about one day calling Easton's family her family.

epilogue

One Week Later

Easton scrambled up the last boulder leading to the summit then reached down to help Lani do the same. A gray haze hovered over the low mountain range to the east of them, and the scattered cumulus clouds had begun to turn orange and pink. They'd arrived right on time.

He kept hold of Lani's hand as they walked up the last small rise, then he shrugged off his backpack and pulled out some blankets, muffins, bananas, and juice. Lani helped him spread out the blanket, and they sat down just as the sun's warm glow began to light the skies.

Not far from his family's home, this hike had always been a favorite of Easton's. He wanted to share it with Lani before she flew back to Maui tomorrow. Cora had insisted that she could manage without her indefinitely, but Lani had been taking care of the business side of the B&B for so long, she knew she needed to be the one to train Maaike.

"I need at least a couple weeks there, and then . . . I guess we'll figure it out after that," she'd said a few days earlier, her eyes filled with uncertainty.

But Easton already had it figured out. He'd had it figured out from the moment he saw her standing on his doorstep in Boston. Which is another reason he'd prodded her awake before the sun and dragged her up here to watch it rise.

"So this is the hike that Facebook and Instagram shared with the world, huh?" she said as she ate a banana. "I can see why. The views are beautiful, especially at this time of day. Everything looks golden."

"In another month, it'll be even more golden when all the leaves began to change. Now *that* is a stunning view." He brushed the crumbs of a muffin off his lap. "To be honest, I understand your feelings about Kapu Aina more than you think. Although it's nice to see people enjoy this particular trail, I'm still a little miffed that we have to come at this hour if we want it all to ourselves."

She set the banana peel on the ground and pulled her knees against her chest, curling her arms around them. "I don't want to leave tomorrow," she said, resting her cheek on the top of her knees so she faced him. "We haven't really talked about when we'll see each other again, and I hate not knowing how long it will be. Promise me we'll work things out soon."

"Why not work them out right now?" Easton slipped his hand into the front pocket of his backpack and closed his fingers around his late-grandmother's diamond ring. As her only grandson, she'd given Easton the ring two days before she'd passed away, telling him to keep it for his future wife. Easton had placed it in a small wooden box in the top drawer of his dresser, where it had stayed until this morning.

Now he clutched it in his fist, trying to remember some of the words he'd been rehearsing for the past week. He drew in a shaky breath, and his palms began to sweat. He didn't usually get nervous or anxious, but he suddenly felt like he was standing on the edge of the Grand Canyon, mustering the courage to leap while praying Lani would be willing to jump with him.

"Everything okay?" Lani asked, her expression worried. "I'm not trying to pressure you or anything. I mean, if you're not ready to make immediate plans, I understand. It's just—"

"Lani."

"Yeah?"

"Will you marry me?" he blurted. It wasn't eloquent, he wasn't down on one knee, and the ring was still clenched in his sweaty hand. But the question had flown out regardless.

She lifted her head from her knees and stared at him, eyes wide, mouth partially open.

He was botching this big-time. Easton tried to slow his breathing, so he could think and formulate some words into sentences. But his mind was a whirlpool, every word being sucked down into a dark abyss.

Get down on one knee, came the first coherent thought. So Easton rolled to his knees in front of Lani and pried his fingers open. "I know it's fast. I know you're not expecting this. And I know I should have probably said something before now, but—"

"Yes!" Lani threw her arms around him, nearly knocking him over. He had enough presence of mind to close his fingers around the ring, so it didn't fly away. And then she was kissing him, hungrily and happily. Easton's future had never felt so bright.

Overhead, the sun continued to rise, like the promise of a wonderful new beginning.

Lani finally pulled back, half laughing and half crying as Easton slid the slightly too-big ring on her trembling finger. "It was my grandmother's," he explained. "The day she gave it to me, she told me that someday I'd meet a woman I'd want to spend the rest of my life with, and that I should give this to her when the time was right. She said you'd be the only daughter-in-law and might feel like an outsider at times, so she wanted you to have this ring so you'd know that she would have loved you like her own granddaughter."

Lani's other hand flew to her mouth. She pressed it against her lips before waving it in front of her face like a fan. Tears leaked from the corners of her eyes and down her cheeks, glinting in the sunlight.

"I'm sorry," she sniffed. "I'm just really . . . happy. I love the ring. It's beautiful and special and . . . means a lot. Mahalo."

Easton smiled, wiping the tears from her eyes. "So it's a yes, then."

"Yes. Of course it's a yes. I already told you it's a yes."

"Good, because I think my mom is already planning the wedding. She adores you, you know."

"Tell her to plan away. I don't care about colors, or food, or decorations or anything. I'd just like it to be in Hāna, if that's okay."

"It's more than okay."

He took Lani's face in his hands and really looked at her. A whiff of apple and wildflowers took him back to the first day he'd met her, when she'd asked him to climb through the window to get into the bungalow.

And then he remembered Samah's words, spoken to him so long ago.

To exchange hearts is beautiful and lovely. It makes you feel . . . more than full. Bigger than yourself.

Easton hadn't understood the words at the time, but it made perfect sense to him now. He'd experienced many things in his short life. He'd stood at the peak of Tavan Bogd, had come face to face with a shark thirty meters under in Palau, and had bathed with elephants in the Cuando River. He'd felt the heady rush of adrenalin, the awe of unsurpassed beauty, and the wonder of colors, mixtures, and diversity. But as he knelt on the top of this peak, looking into the eyes of his future, he realized that all of his prior experiences were only a flattened version of what they could have been. Lani had made his world round, and he would always love her for it.

Dear Reader,

Thanks so much for reading! This has been a fun project to work on, and I hope you enjoy all the other books in the Power of the Matchmaker series. All the contributing authors are wonderful writers and people.

If you're interested in being notified of new releases, feel free to sign up for my New Release mailing list on my website at RachaelReneeAnderson.com (will only be used to email you about new releases).

Also, if can spare a few minutes, I'd love a review from you on Goodreads, Amazon or wherever else you'd care to post one.

Thanks again for your support and happy reading!

Rachael

Other Books by Rachael Anderson

USA TODAY BESTSELLING AUTHOR OF CLEAN ROMANCE

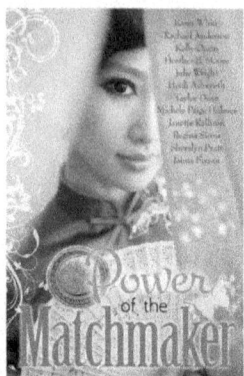

12 Novels *by* 12 bestselling authors *in* 12 months

Kami White
Rachael Anderson
Kelly Oram
Heather B. Moore
Julie Wright
Heidi Ashworth
Taylor Dean
Michele Paige Holmes
Janette Rallison
Regina Sirois
Sheralyn Pratt
Jaima Fixsen

Power

of the

Matchmaker

—SERIES—

November 2015... *Power of the Matchmaker*
(A prequel novella of the Matchmaker's story)

January 1, 2016

February 1, 2016

March 1, 2016

April 1, 2016

May 1, 2016

June 1, 2016

July 1, 2016

August 1, 2016

September 1, 2016

October 1, 2016

November 1, 2016

December 1, 2016

Available for Purchase or Pre order in Power of the Matchmaker

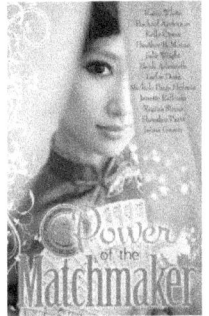

Read the matchmaker's story (prequel novella) to find out where it all starts . . .

Mae Li has been in love with Chen Zhu for years, and he with her. But when the matchmaker arrives at the Zhu family home, she recommends another village girl for Chen.

Heartbroken, Mae Li flees her village with the clothes on her back and her only possession—a pearl embedded comb, given to her as a goodbye gift from Chen Zhu.

Upon Mae's arrival in Shanghai, she quickly learns that she'll starve within days unless she sells her prized comb or joins a courtesan house. But when Ms. Tan, the matchmaker of Shanghai, finds Mae, her life will be forever changed.

꙳

Celia is in desperate need of a change—a change of scenery, a change of pace, and a complete redo of all relationships. Not

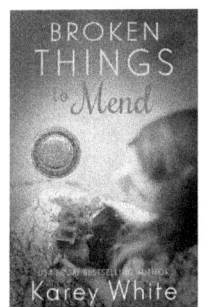

knowing what else to do, she opens a map, closes her eyes, and lets fate decide her future. Then she packs her meager belongings and buys a one-way ticket to a little town on the fringes of Oregon's Deschutes National Forest called Sisters. She's wanted a family for years. Will she find one in Sisters?

What Celia doesn't plan to find is a strange Chinese woman whose meddling ways keep throwing her in the path of a handsome, but reserved, forest ranger. But no matter how kind or dependable Silas seems to be, there are some things in Celia's past that neither of them can escape, and this time, the damage might be too much to mend.

Music meets Movies in this sweet college romance from the bestselling author of *Cinder & Ella*.

NYU freshman Nate Anderson is a triplet who is desperate to escape his wild and crazy brothers. After they screw things up for him one too many times, Nate flees his housing situation and takes the first available room for rent as far from his brothers as he can get.

Enter his new roommate Jordan—a quirky LA girl who believes that everything in life has already been done in the movies. In this heartfelt tale of love, friendship and family, Nate learns how to deal with his new adult life using Hollywood films as a guide.

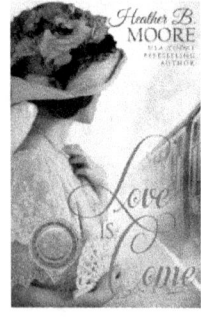

Nelle Thompson lives a life of privilege during the turn of the century New York City. When her parents are killed in a terrible accident, she's forced to live with her aunt's family in a small town in Connecticut, and treated as a poor relation with no financial independence. Broken hearted and riddled with insomnia, Nelle's health begins a downward spiral. When a locked part of her heart blossoms around her cousin's fiancé Mathew Janson, Nelle doesn't know if she can endure one more heartbreak. Miss Pearl, owner of the local apothecary shop, becomes a mother figure to Nelle, but a fateful summer day has Nelle questioning everything she's ever believed and wondering if she'll ever love again.

About Rachael Anderson

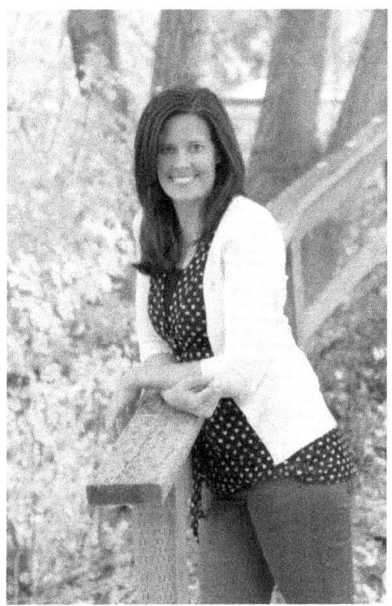

Rachael Anderson is a *USA Today* bestselling author and mother of four crazy, but awesome kids. Over the years she's gotten pretty good at breaking up fights or at least sending guilty parties to their rooms. She can't sing, doesn't dance, and despises tragedies, but she recently figured out how yeast works and can now make homemade bread, which she is really good at eating. You can read more about her and her books online at RachaelReneeAnderson.com.

Acknowledgements

First and foremost, I have to thank Karey White and Heather Moore, for being excited and willing to team up with me on this project. They're both creative, brilliant, and so very fun to work with. And a special thanks to Karey for editing my book for me.

Braden, as always, thank you for your thorough, honest critique, while still being encouraging at the same time.

Andrea, thank you, thank you, thank you for your valuable feedback and for catching all that you did. I'm indebted to you big-time.

Rebecca, thank you for your keen eye and for being willing to take time out of your busy schedule to help me out. I'm so grateful!

Karen, thank you for being willing to beta read and proof my book. I'm so grateful for your help and willingness to do that!

Jeff—yet again, a hundred million thanks for being the husband, father, and friend that you are. I love you.

And, as always, I have to thank my heavenly father, for loving me enough to challenge and bless me.

www.ingramcontent.com/pod-product-compliance
Lightning Source LLC
Chambersburg PA
CBHW071500170626
46811CB00007B/2646